BROKEN ALLIANCE

VALLA SERIES ~ BOOK FOUR

ANNA REZES

WORDS
IMAGINED

ALSO BY ANNA REZES

VALLA SERIES:
Unraveling Emily ~ book one
Descendant of Valla ~ book two
Guardian of Latovia ~ book three
The Thorn ~ Novella 3.5
Broken Alliance ~ book four

Pink f*cking Moscato

ISBN: 978-1-950657-15-5 (paperback)

ISBN: 978-1-950657-16-2 (hardcover)

Library of Congress Control Number: 2020904654

This is a work of fiction. Names, characters, places, and incidents are either a product of the author's imagination or are used fictitiously. Any resemblance to actual persons, living or dead, events, or locales is entirely coincidental.

Cover design by German Creative

First Edition:

Words Imagined

Hilliard, OH

www.annarezes.com

To Cathy Kline, who was an integral part of bringing the Valla Series to life.

PROLOGUE

Six months ago

LATHE LIT UP HIS PHONE, holding it out to see in front of him. He found his mother curled up on the floor by the sofa in her modified basement apartment. She whimpered when the light illuminated her features.

"Mother, what do you see?"

"Gore," Evelyn whispered, uncurling from the fetal position to look at him with cloudy eyes. "Gore . . . and an army of horned beasts and fire. Fire burning everything." Her eyes grew wider as if what she was seeing was happening right in front of her. "Fire burning everything!" She folded back into a ball, covering her head with her arms. "No, no, no, no, no, no, no."

Lathe breathed out a sigh and put his phone away. He crouched to sit on the floor next to her, his back resting against the side of the sofa while he placed a reassuring hand on his mother's back, hoping she was only having a delusion and not a vision of the future, but he knew better. Delusions didn't incite such an emotional reaction from her. Lathe knew something bad was coming, but how could he possibly prepare when the details were so vague.

DRAGONS

1

FIRE RAINS down from the heavens as winged demons fly through the night sky, exhaling flames. Opposed to other fabled dragons, these creatures are without scales and their slimy skin shimmers in the firelight. The mansion and stables burn while frightened horses run wild across the vast landscape. In the center of the chaos, riding fearlessly on the back of a snow-white horse is the scarred face of a warrior. Lathe shouts at the night sky, his face contorting with anger as he lashes out with violent winds.

Emily's blond hair flows out behind her, her beautiful face dusted with soot and streaked with tears as she comes from the woods riding on the back of a giant horned elk. Following her is a horde of horned beasts leaping out of the woods. She joins up with Lathe in the meadow just as a hippo sized dragon swoops down from the sky, breathing fire. Emily grabs the horns of her massive elk and rises to her feet on its back. She thrusts her arm out, shooting white-hot flames from her palm. There is no chance for the dragon to dodge the blaze, and as it strikes the beast, its blood-curdling screams penetrate the air, sounding almost human. The creature spirals to the earth, breaking the ground and silencing its cries forever.

Hearing the call of their fallen brother, the dragons swarm, circling the meadow. With stocky necks, thick stubby limbs, and slimy skin, they look like humanoid flying slugs. Their sizes vary, from two-hundred pounds to two-thousand with bat-like wings that span from ten to twenty feet. Dozens of the hideous creatures come from all directions.

Lathe uses the air around him as a weapon, using sharp winds to throw his enemy off course, while Emily uses her gifts to leap onto the back of a deformed dragon flying too close. Her fingers grip onto the viscous skin of the beast, and before it throws her, she melds her mind with it.

Its stench is overwhelming, like a rotting corpse mixed with spoiled milk and mold. She forces the dragon up, flying higher into the sky. Her body slips down the creature as a chunk of the dragon's flesh sloughs off in her hand. She cringes, gagging as she drops the fleshy piece and grabs another area of the beast.

Once she's up high enough, she looks around, searching beyond the burned mansion and plumes of smoke covering the ground. Over the next hill, Emily spots what she's looking for and sends the dragon into a dive.

The mother dragon sits on the hillside looking regal. Its forty-foot wingspan dwarfs the others, and glistening purple and green scales cover its body, making her shimmer. The scales make the dragons flame-retardant, but none of the other dragons have them.

Emily dives through the sky, silent except for her heartbeat hammering. She realizes her dragon's stench is giving her away as the scaled beast's nostrils flare, sniffing twice before turning to face her. She swerves to the side, and her dragon loses its balance and spirals. Emily lets go, using the air to cushion her fall, while the deformed beast dies upon impact. These creatures weren't built to last. They were created to kill.

Emily rolls up to her feet, and the ground rumbles as the mother dragon stalks towards her. As it comes closer, Emily notices what she didn't before. On the back of the mother-dragon sits a Latovian warrior. Ashley turns her blond head, pinning Emily with her dark glare.

Emily shouts, "Ashley, don't do this!"

Ashley shakes her head, disgust curling her lips. "You've forced our hand!" She spits, "It's the only option you've left us!"

"Lathe is over there!" Emily warns, shouting to be heard. "Your dragons will kill him!"

Ashley's gaze flicks down for a moment before returning to Emily, her voice vibrating with rage, "Then let him die!"

Ashley yanks on the dragon's reins, and a thunderous rumbling begins inside the beast. Its neck extends toward the night, and its mouth opens, filling the heavens with the fires of hell before turning her flames toward Emily.

Ashley cries out, her triumph tainted with grief.

THE PRESENT COMES BACK to Ashley as a cold sweat breaks out across her skin. It's always a little too chilly down here for her liking, but Latovia stayed a mild fifty to sixty degrees.

Hundreds of years ago, the Olvasho made it so the sun—

the very source of Latovian magic—would kill Latovians should the sun or its shadow touch their skin. So now they are stuck here, in their underground world called Latovia.

The glow of magic gemstones in the cave walls illuminates the room. They still glow gold, the color of Evelyn's magic. Evelyn was half Latovian, half Olvasho, which is how she survived both sides of the portal, but even her immense power didn't stop a bullet from killing her.

Ashley doesn't have an ounce of Olvasho blood, but she has twice the amount of power a Latovian usually holds, which allows her to absorb the sun's energy. At least for now.

She sits on a hard seat with her back ramrod straight, holding her composure. Her visions are coming more frequently, and each time they feel more alive than they did before. She tries to hide her trembling, remaining stoic as the needle repeatedly bites into her wrist.

Latovian tattoos are inscribed without the use of modern technology. Each stick of the needle burns like a swarm of bee stings, because mixed in the tattoo's ink, is Latovian magic.

First, a Latovian gemstone is melted down, the magic extracted and mixed with the ink. Then a custom-made needle, wielded by the precise hand of a carver, pierces the skin over and over again. The process is grueling, taking hours to complete two of the three thin bands around Ashley's wrist. She stays strong through the first two bands but feels faint by the end of the third.

"We'll finish in the morning," Wolfe announces in his gravelly voice. He speaks a little more stern, using the voice of authority—the voice of a king. People don't question him.

The carver is already packing up supplies. Ashley's

shoulders stay rigid, her posture perfect as the surrounding group ready themselves to leave. Wolfe stands across from Ashley as everyone files out. His nearly black eyes meet hers, communicating understanding and compassion. His ebony skin and long dreadlocks almost match his black dragon skin jacket and pants. He looks like a shadow—one you wouldn't want to cross in a dark alley.

When Wolfe was sixteen, he killed the previous king, not in the traditional battle challenge, but by slicing the king's throat as he slept. What Wolfe did was ruthless, illegal, and punishable by death, but it didn't stop the Latovian people from demanding Wolfe take kingship. He was the only Latovian king voted into his role.

Wolfe closes the door after the last person exits the room. As soon as he flips the lock, Ashley's shoulders slump, her head falling back, while she lets go of her tears. Wolfe walks over to her, encouraging, "You did good today."

She lifts her head to glare at him, her inky eyes furious. "These traditions are barbaric."

"It is the Latovian way."

"That doesn't mean it's right!"

"No, but traditions take time to break. You didn't cry. They will respect you more for your bravery."

Strands of platinum blond hair fall in her face as she inspects the simple black lines around her wrist. She expects her skin to be swollen and red, but her pale skin is unblemished, marked only with the delicate tattooed bracelets around her wrist.

She pushes her long hair back, tucking it behind her ear as she looks up at Wolfe. "Can I go?" She presses her full lips together as she stares up at him with glistening eyes.

He steps back, out of her way. "The tattoo is not complete, but I'm not holding you here."

She wipes her tears as she stands. "Where is Deja?"

"I told her to stay with him."

Deja is Lathe's favorite Latovian, aside from Ashley. The eight-year-old has more courage and gumption than any adult Ashley has met. Her spirit seems unbreakable, especially given the way her life began. When Deja was a toddler, her father challenged Wolfe in a fight to the death. When Deja's father lost, Deja's mother was ashamed and took Deja with her as she walked out into the sunlight. The sunlight killed Deja's mother instantly as the curse the Olvasho placed against those with Latovian blood burned through her body. Children were immune to the curse, so after Deja watched her mother die, she found shelter in the stables behind the Vallor mansion. Lathe was the one who found and cared for her until Wolfe came to retrieve her during the new moon—the only time the Latovian curse is suspended. Lathe handed Deja over, but the two had already bonded, and their bond had only grown over the years.

Wolfe walks Ashley to the portal door. She has not yet completely succumbed to her Latovian blood, but things are getting worse, and she knows it is only a matter of time until she can no longer leave Latovia.

Before she walks out of the portal, Wolfe reminds her, "Set your timer. Remember to watch your tattoos."

She nods. "See you soon," she says, holding back the tears that always threaten.

Lathe and Deja are right outside the portal, waiting on her. The once dank, unwelcoming tunnel below the mansion had become a livable space thanks to Lathe's hard work. The biggest problem is its massive size. The arched stone ceiling above them is easily thirty feet high, and the tunnel itself is the size of a football field. Yet, Lathe works tirelessly on the space to make it more comfortable for Ashley.

Deja runs to Ashley. Her jet-black hair and eyes nearly as dark are stark in contrast to her pale skin. She is tiny for an eight-year-old, but her size only makes her more fierce.

Ashley thinks she's going to get a hug, but Deja pushes Ashley's sleeve up to view the new black bands around her wrist. "So cool! I can't wait to get my own," she says, looking at her own wrists.

Ashley barely holds back her wince. The day she gets her tattoo will be the day she can't come visit Lathe anymore, and she's afraid that will hurt him even more than her own absence.

"You still have some time, Deja. Enjoy your freedom while you have it," Ashley reminds her.

Deja wraps her little arms around Ashley in a quick hug, before leaving through the portal door.

Ashley finds Lathe staring at her from ten feet away. His tall, lean body sags against the wall, and his shaved scalp hides beneath the hood of his sweatshirt. She wonders if he'll ever stop trying to hide. Others may call him intimidating or sinister because of the horrific scars along the left side of his face and torso, but all Ashley sees is the beautiful man she fell in love with. Without his scars, she fears he would be too pretty. She loves every rough part of him, and the scars speak volumes about what kind of man he is. He was a teenager when he deformed himself in order to save his mother. It was one of many sacrifices. He has spent his whole life protecting those who can't defend themselves.

Seeing him now reminds Ashley of the vision she had earlier—the vision of him riding horseback across a burning lawn with dragons flying above.

Her visions began shortly after Evelyn died. She didn't think much of them at first. She thought they were just vivid daydreams, completely inconsequential. But then her little daydreams started coming to life. They were little snippets of reality before they happened. Now her visions have grown elaborate and ominous.

Lathe's eyes don't miss a thing as he pushes away from the wall. "You had the vision again?"

She nods, her eyes blurring.

He steps toward her, pulling her against his chest. She takes in his scent as her fingers claw into his back, holding onto him as if it will hold off the inevitable.

Visions of the future were Evelyn's thing, but when Evelyn accidentally killed Ashley, she merged their souls to save Ashley's life. Now Ashley sees pieces of the future.

"What are we gonna do, Lathe?"

FRAGILE

2

Ominous clouds blanketed the May sky, threatening showers. The ground, over-saturated from a week's worth of rain, squishes beneath Patrick's boots as he walks through the lush green lawn from the Fort Wayne mansion to the stables around back. The pasture is rife with spring noises. Crickets chirp, birds sing, and insects buzz by as Patrick tromps through the high grass. If he had realized sooner how tall the grass was, he would have taken the driveway back. He swats at a bug before pulling his hood up over his short blond waves as it begins to rain.

He looks ahead, spotting Lathe outside on the far side of the barn. Lathe's boots nearly get stuck in the mud as he leads his snow-white horse toward the barn. Deja, perched on the back of the mare, notices Patrick. She points, and Lathe turns to look. Lathe switches direction, moving toward Patrick.

They meet just outside the barn doors, but before Patrick speaks, the rain stops and wind stills. The chirping birds grow silent, and the crickets stop their song. The fine hairs on the back of his neck rise, and he looks across the lush pasture to the mansion, noting, "Emily's awake."

Deja asks, "How do you know?"

"The wind stopped," Lathe says.

"Don't you feel the stillness? The silence?" Patrick asks, rubbing a hand over his angular jaw, noticing the stubble he'd been ignoring. Shaving had fallen down his list of priorities when Emily started falling apart.

Deja takes in her surroundings and shivers. "That's creepy."

"How's she doing?" Lathe asks.

Patrick drops his hand. "Worse," he answers without elaborating.

Lathe shakes his head. "You shouldn't have told her about Ashley's vision."

Patrick scowls. "I can't keep that from her."

Emily's hold over the air around them snaps, and the rain resumes.

Patrick shifts his focus to Deja. "Have you gotten anything from Wolfe?"

She slides a glance at Lathe before saying, "If there were dragons, I would know about them, okay. I know all the things I'm not supposed to know."

"Well, then how do you explain Ashley's vision?" Patrick asks, spinning toward Lathe, "You guys raised Deja to be a spy. How do we trust her? The Olvasho are Latovia's sworn enemy."

Lathe feels the surge of power pulling from Patrick and readies himself in response.

Deja jumps down from the horse, a sloppy dismount, but

she always lands on her feet. She's like a cat in that way. She steps right up to Patrick, her recent growth spurt bringing her face level with his chest. "You want to interrogate me? Go ahead. I won't crack!"

Lathe snorts, "Is that what you've stooped to, Patrick. Interrogating children?" He shakes his head.

Patrick scoffs, "She's hardly a child. I'm starting to think Latovia doesn't have children. They force their babies into adulthood, leaving toddlers to fend for themselves."

Lathe pulls Deja back as he steps forward. "The Olvasho aren't much better."

"Pathetic." Jerrick's deep baritone grabs everyone's attention as he comes out of the barn, his large frame filling the doorway. "You guys are turning on each other because of the unsubstantiated claims of a dead woman." He pulls his hood over his dark buzzed hair and his piercing blue eyes narrow on the group.

Most Olvasho have blond hair, blue eyes, fair skin, and extraordinary beauty. Jerrick has the blue eyes and the looks with his perfectly symmetrical face and the physique of an Olympian God, but with his dark hair and chocolate skin, he broke the Olvasho mold.

Everyone noticed him, so over the years, he found a way to cloak his looks. He didn't change or distort himself, but mentally he made it difficult for people to focus on his distinct features unless they really looked hard.

At twenty-four, he is older than the others. He originally signed on to help Emily know the ins and out of the Olvasho world, but now his most important role has become peacekeeper. "I know Emily's mother must have believed what she put in her journals, but there is no proof, and until there is, we will continue to work with the Latovian people."

Patrick folds his arms over his chest with a smirk. "Were those Emily's orders?"

Face twisting in irritation, Jerrick shifts his full attention to Patrick before copying his stance by folding his massive arms against his chest. His muscles bulge, looking as if they will split the seam of his shirt. Despite the menacing appearance, his voice stays calm. "Ashley and Deja are Latovian. Hell, even Lathe is one-fourth Latovian. We are a team—a family. We don't turn on each other because of a rumor, no matter its source. Not until we have reason to believe it's true."

Patrick drops his arms before running a hand through his hair. "And what about Ashley's visions?"

"They are one version of the future," Jerrick answers. "One possibility in an endless number of futures. But forcing Latovia to defend themselves against us and feeding them this dragon bullshit will only cause them to want to fight us and put ideas in their heads."

"It's too late for that," Patrick snickers. "Ashley already told Wolfe about the visions."

It begins to pour, so Jerrick steps back, letting Patrick and Deja step into the barn while Lathe takes his horse around to the stable doors.

In the barn, Jerrick places a hand on Patrick's shoulder. "Why are you trying to start a fight? You are closer to Emily than any of us. Calm her mind instead of letting her rile you up. We're all worried about her. I'll listen to our Vezetö, no matter her orders, but right now, she needs advice, and I know I am her adviser, but she listens to you."

Patrick takes a deep breath, trying to loosen his muscles, but it's useless, pointless. She has him all wrapped up, and the dragons have him worried. He doesn't know how much longer he can be the stable one.

PATRICK TRAVELS up to Emily's room, his hair and clothing damp from the rain. He knows Emily is a disaster, only functioning when people are watching. She's the head of the Olvasho, but right now, it is just a show. She went nonstop for weeks after Evelyn died, and then she read her mother's journal.

It stopped her dead in her tracks. It was the thing that finally broke her. And her breakdown couldn't have come at a worse time.

Patrick knocks at Emily's bedroom door and stands there a moment, waiting for an answer that never comes. He tries the handle. Finding it unlocked, he opens the door slowly and finds her lounging in the window seat with her back to him. Her head is propped in her hand, her tangle of greasy blond hair spread out behind her. Maggie is on the floor beside her, on high alert, a loyal companion until the end. Though Patrick had watched after Maggie for months while Emily struggled with Adelaide, now that the spirits are gone, Maggie doesn't leave Emily's side unless instructed otherwise.

"Emily," Patrick says as he steps into the room.

With no response from her, he moves toward Emily. Maggie growls, low and menacing. Her lips peel back, showing teeth.

"Really, Maggie?" He moves forward.

Maggie's warning gets louder. Her chest rumbles, and she stands from her haunches, her hackles rising.

Patrick lowers a hand, letting his magic flow from himself to the dog. "Shh."

Maggie recognizes his magic and whimpers, sitting back, her hair raised but her teeth hidden. Patrick continues forward. He knows Emily has trouble sleeping these days, and when she does finally fall asleep, she wakes screaming from the nightmares that constantly haunt her.

He walks cautiously to the window, calling her name the whole way, speaking softly, so he doesn't upset Maggie. As he gets closer, he pets the dog, and she seems to relax but doesn't move from her watch.

Patrick peeks over Emily's shoulder to see her eyes fixed on the window, not just looking out, but looking beyond anything visible. She's looking into the past. Adelaide, her evil ancestor and essentially the creator of the Olvasho, possessed her mind for months, filling her with memories that deeply disturb her. When Emily finally rid her mind of Adelaide, Valla, the first of her bloodline disappeared from her mind too. Emily didn't realize how much she relied on Valla until she was gone. Now, without Valla to help her cope, she's falling apart.

Patrick places a hand on her shoulder, and she jerks, flipping towards him. White-hot flames shoot from both her palms. He jumps back, barely missing the flash that sets the bed on fire. Patrick pulls moisture from the air and douses the fire, soaking Emily's bed and containing the flames.

Emily is on her feet, her breaths coming heavy and loud, her chest rising and falling as she attempts to calm herself.

Her emerald eyes are wide, red-rimmed, and bloodshot. Wisps of blond hair fall across her pale face, and she's wearing the same dirty, wrinkled clothes she had on yesterday and the day before.

His heart breaks to see her like this. This past year hasn't been kind to her. She is far from the naive girl he found a year ago. She's seen so much death, so much evil, and has experienced too much bad to believe in good. Ben gave her hope. He made her believe in goodness, but since they broke up, everything has gone downhill, and since the nightmares began, she has not been the same.

He stares cautiously, waiting her out. Her behavior has been dangerously unpredictable, and he's not sure what to say to her.

She stands up straight and pushes her hair out of her face, glaring at him. "Stop looking at me like that."

Patrick lifts his hand in a gesture of surrender. "Like what? Like I'm concerned?"

Her eyes narrow. "Like I'm broken beyond repair."

"That is not what I'm doing."

She sighs loudly and turns away from him. "You used to want me. Now you just feel sorry for me."

"Emily—"

She spins back, shouting, "I dare you to deny it!"

He closes his eyes, searching for some composure. Blowing out a breath, he looks at her, saying, "Emily, nobody knows how to talk to you anymore. You haven't changed clothes or showered in days. You barely sleep. You barely eat. You're paranoid, and half the time, you're not even in control of your gifts. I know you're grieving and scared—"

"I am not scared!"

"Yes, you are." He steps closer. "And that's okay. You're not in this alone."

"Yes, I am." She spins away from him, wandering toward the window. "Nobody sees the things I see. Nobody has the memories I have. I am alone."

She pivots, watching her socked feet move across the hardwood floor, careful to avoid the cracks while she mumbles, "The Olvasho, the very people I try to protect banded together to form a team that tried to kill me. Evelyn let herself be killed. I'm supposed to free the Latovian people, despite them possessing more power than we can imagine. Despite the fact that they could kill us all." She tosses her arms out as she continues to watch the floorboards. "I don't know who to trust anymore. I don't even know which ideas are my own."

Hysterical laughter bubbles out of her. "My life has been a carefully constructed operation since birth. My mom had an agenda that even my dad didn't know about. It's the reason we moved to Ohio. Every coincidence, every decision I thought I made on my own has been a carefully thought-out manipulation plotted by my mother."

"Where are you getting this from?" he asks, stepping into her line of sight.

She looks up at him. "My dad sent me more journal entries." Pushing him out of the way, she continues her methodical movements back and forth across the room. "She had to be working with Evelyn. She wrote things about the future that have already come true. Most of the journal is written in riddles and rhymes, which is why my dad didn't understand them, but she never wrote Ashley's name. She called her Latovia's gem."

Patrick wonders if this is true, or something she made up in her head. "Where are these journals?"

She points toward the bed where she'd left loose printed pages spread across the comforter. "First, I was supposed to meet Ashley at school, but they split the districts differently, so we didn't meet. Then the contingency plans kicked in."

Patrick pulls a sheet of paper from the stack on the bed. Half of the ink smeared page has burned away, and what remains is illegible as it drips inky water on the hardwood.

Seeing the paper in his hand, she says, "The original is in my email." She goes back to pacing. "First contingency was my dad's office party at Ashley's family's country club, but I refused to go, so we didn't meet. There are a dozen different scenarios my mom outlined in her journals, so even if I hadn't met Ashley at work, we would have met somehow.

"I don't know why my mom thought we'd hit it off, but she wanted us to be friends. In her goodbye note to me, she said I'd be the one to end this feud. I thought she was talking about Sky, but what if she wasn't? What if she was talking about the feud between the Olvasho and Latovian people? I think she knew I'd end up leading the Olvasho, and she knew Ashley was a Latovian princess. She made sure that our paths would cross, just like she knew I would meet you. Even from the grave, she manipulated everything."

Patrick tilts his head. "I want to see these journals."

"Because you don't believe me?"

"Because I'm skeptical of everything and like to see with my own eyes." He steps forward and despite her little step backward, he pulls her into a hug. She doesn't fight him, but she doesn't reciprocate.

Against his chest, she whispers, "Everything is changing, Patrick."

He rests his head against hers. "I know, and everything will continue to change because that's how the world works."

She steps out of his embrace. "What do we do about the dragons?"

"We don't even know if they exist."

She looks up at him. "But we do, between my mother's words and Ashley's visions, they have to be real."

"We don't understand Ashley's visions. Maybe she's seeing what she fears. No Latovian children are missing, so we know the dragons—if they are real—are not feeding on kids like your mom wrote in her last journal of mad ramblings."

"They aren't all mad, and do they even keep track of all their orphans?"

His voice softens. "Ashley is keeping track of them. She cares about those kids, and according to her, so do Lathe and Wolfe."

She spins away from him. "Wolfe has a funny way of showing it, letting them sleep on slabs of rocks, unguarded, unprotected. They have nothing!"

Patrick sighs. "He makes sure they get fed, and he makes sure they have clothes. They may go unsupervised, but Ashley says the orphans are a unit. They look out for each other."

"They're kids, Patrick!"

"You've seen Deja. She's a Latovian orphan. Does she act like a kid to you?"

"We need to send someone down there to spy. I'd do it myself if the curse wasn't deadly for Olvasho."

"It's too dangerous to send someone in, and it'd break their trust."

"We could send Morgan in or Alec. He's been there before. The curse wouldn't hurt them since they don't have Olvasho abilities. They'd be safe down there."

"No."

"I'm not saying to do it. I'm just saying—"

"No," he states, "I won't put them in danger."

"You were never that cautious with me."

He closes his eyes. "And look what happened to you."

She steps toward him. "Patrick, did you know there are Elk farms in Indiana? I didn't until I looked it up because I've never even seen an elk in real life, but they keep showing up in Ashley's vision. So, I wanted to see what they look like. I called the elk farm to see if any are missing. They deny it, but it could happen. Anything can happen." She grabs his shirt. "I need sleep, Patrick. I need it so badly."

He peeks at her bed, black and charred. "We'll have to get a new bed for you."

"No."

He smirks. "Would you prefer a cement slab in solidarity to the Latovian orphans?"

"I would prefer your room, Patrick."

He waits for her to continue explaining her request, but she just stares at him, looking as if she is about to cry.

"What's changed, Emily?"

"Forget it." She turns away. "You're disgusted by me, treating me like a fragile child, instead of a—"

He places a hand on her shoulder and spins her back toward him. "Love, just because you're fragile right now, doesn't mean you're undesirable."

"You're the only person who is brave enough and maybe crazy enough to do what I need. I mean, I could've turned you into a human shish kabob, and I shouldn't even ask you, but I'm asking anyway. Let me sleep in your room."

He watches her for a moment, hesitant.

"These nightmares are . . . Patrick the things Adelaide has done and the things these Latovian's might be doing to their children . . ." She shakes her head and wipes her sweaty hands on her pants. "Nevermind, it's stupid and dangerous. I'm not thinking clearly. I'm sorry, Patrick. I think I need to be alone."

"You need to shower, love."

"I know. You're right. I just have no energy," she says, sagging onto the window seat.

KEEPING SECRETS

3

Morgan knocks as she enters Alec and Cindy's house the way she's done a thousand times before. The deep bark alerts her that Molly and Ben are already there with their massive dog. The brown fluff of fur rushes up to Morgan, covering her in slobbery kisses. The Newfoundland is well over one-hundred pounds, and Morgan is happy he doesn't jump on her like he did at last Sunday's "family" dinner.

"Max!" Molly calls, coming around the corner from the kitchen at the back of the house. She walks through the living room into the foyer. "Hey, Morgan. We're having meatloaf tonight."

Ben turns around on the couch, looking at Morgan with wide eyes and shaking his head. Molly's back is to him as he says, "Molly made the dinner tonight!" His tone is pleasant, but his warning is clear.

"Ben, I can see you in the door's reflection. Asshole, it's not gross!"

"Language!" Cindy yells from the kitchen. She'd sort of adopted Ben and Molly after their parents got arrested on a multitude of criminal charges.

"Shit," Molly whispers and hugs Morgan.

Morgan still can't believe the change in the sixteen-year-old. She was a far cry from the bitchy girl she met months ago. It's amazing what love and nurturing can do.

When Molly pulls away, she whispers conspiratorially, "I have a boyfriend."

"Connor or Andrew?" Morgan whispers back.

"Neither. His name is Bryn. He's—"

"A dead man when Ben finds out," Alec says, coming out from his room.

"Alec, he's being crazy, and you know it. I'm not stupid. I can take care of myself."

"And he has every right to want to protect you," Alec says.

"It's not like I'm dating someone like you," Molly says, "Bryn isn't a player."

Alec calls out, "Ben, Molly has a boyfriend, some guy named Bryan."

"His name is Bryn, not Bryan."

Ben stands from the couch. "Why haven't I heard this?" He's always been protective of Molly, but since he became her guardian, Morgan feels he's become a tad overprotective.

As the siblings fight, Morgan elbows Alec. "Why'd you do that?"

Alec wears a mischievous smile. "I have something I want to show you." He turns toward his room, and she follows him inside. He closes the door while she looks around his room.

She turns back to him, saying, "Nope, it looks the same as last time."

"Oh, that's right, you've already seen the new curtains." With a smile, he crosses the small room like he can't stand being so far away. "I keep forgetting."

She leans against his desk saying, "I mean, I'm sure there is something new in here, maybe like a new pen or maybe—"

His arms wrap around her, but she pulls back, complaining, "Alec."

He kisses the smooth skin of her neck, and she melts into him. "Alec," she says again, her tone soft as she lifts her chin and their mouths meet.

Keeping their new development a secret hasn't been easy. Still, the timing is tricky, and they want a little while to adjust to their new relationship without hearing opinions and judgments from others.

Morgan pulls back. "We can't do this here. Why don't you come over later?"

Morgan inherited Patrick's apartment. He said he didn't want to get rid of it, but Morgan knows he has very little reason to be in Columbus these days. She offered to take over his rent, but he insists on paying. Fine with her. She's a broke college student so she'll accept the freebie from her super loaded cousin.

"I can't. I'm still working mandatory overtime. And work is still mad at me for missing that day when the Olvasho tried to kill us."

"I thought Jerrick smoothed everything over."

He shrugs. "I didn't get fired."

"Have you told Ben about it?"

"Hell no. He doesn't need to hear that shit."

"Do you have to cuss all the time?"

"Do you have to breathe?" he asks with a smirk.

"You're comparing your curse words to breathing now?"

He leans in, kissing the tip of her nose. "I'll try to cut back."

"I don't want to change you. I don't want to be that girl-friend that makes you change everything about yourself, and I'm not telling you to stop, just cut back. Dang it, I'm still doing it!"

Alec cups her cheeks and smiles as he kisses her. "It's fine, dear. I'll change the very essence of my vocabulary."

She pulls back with a laugh. "Stop it."

"Stop what? I shan't upset the lady. This is just how I shall speak from now unto eternity."

"Oh, so this is going to be a thing?"

He places his hand over his heart. "Heavens no, not a thing."

Morgan shakes her head and rolls her eyes. "They're going to notice we're missing."

"Then let us go eat thy questionable loaf of meat prepared with love."

Morgan moves past him, toward the door. "I'm gonna kill you."

"Morgan, you mustn't speak of such violence."

She waves her hand toward him. "This is not what I was talking about. I don't know who you're trying to imitate right now. No one talks like that."

"That hurts my feelings, Morgan. I shall only be my best self from here onward."

Morgan rolls her eyes again and walks out of his room.

The arguing siblings have moved to the living room. Ben is talking into Molly's bright purple cell phone while Molly is lying back on the couch, her hands covering her face, mumbling threats under her breath.

Ben says, "Great, looking forward to meeting you, Bryn." He hangs up and drops the phone in her lap.

She jerks up to a sitting position. "I cannot believe you just did that!"

Ben notices Morgan and Alec and says, "I invited Bryn to dinner."

Morgan's eyes grow wide. "Ben, you didn't." She gives Molly a sympathetic look.

Ben shrugs. "I want to meet him."

Molly shakes her head, looking at her phone. "My life is over." She stands suddenly and to Ben, says, "You're the worst!"

"Stop being so dramatic," Ben sighs.

She grunts, stomping her foot. "I can't with you. I can't even."

Alec speaks up, "Goodness me, did you hear, Morgan? Molly currently does not possess the ability to can."

Morgan closes her eyes, while Molly glares at Alec, and Ben gives him a questioning look.

Then Cindy comes from the kitchen. "What time will Bryn be here?"

"His mom is going to drop him off any minute. Apparently, they live close."

"Ugh, Ben!" Molly cries.

"Molly, hun, it's going to be fine. Ben will be nice to your boyfriend. He just wants to meet him."

"Yeah, because he suddenly thinks he's my dad," Molly storms off, going into Alec's bedroom and slamming the door.

Morgan looks at Ben. "So how's this guerrilla parenting going for you?"

He takes a deep breath, looking in the direction Molly went. "This is hard. I don't like it. I don't like acting like a parent, but I just graduated. I know how guys that age are. I won't let anything happen to her, and I don't know how else to protect her."

"You could trust her a little," Morgan suggests.

"Maybe next time don't threaten her boyfriend to come to Sunday dinner," Cindy adds.

"I feel you have been gifted, nay, blessed with truly exceptional parental prowess."

Everyone looks at Alec and Ben questions, "What?"

Morgan shrugs. "He thinks he's being funny."

Alec grabs his chest. "You do not appreciate my gesticulations?"

"Your what?"

"My jokes."

Morgan shakes her head. "That's not what gesticulation means."

"Well, smarty-pants, I may not knoweth the words, but I believeth that Molly is climbing out thy windowpane."

"Shit." Ben runs to the front door.

Cindy turns to Morgan and asks, "Did you ask him to stop cussing?"

"I just asked him to cut back."

Cindy nods. "He did the same thing to me when I told him to stop."

A few minutes later, Molly and Ben walk back in the

door, appearing to have struck some sort of truce. Shortly after, Bryn shows up, looking nervous. Morgan whispers to Molly, "He's cute."

Molly nods and goes over to greet her boyfriend, apologizing for her crazy brother.

TORMENT

4

Jᴇʀʀɪᴄᴋ ᴡᴀᴋᴇs out of a dead sleep. His lights are flickering, and the unease in the air has him getting out of bed. Something feels wrong. Vast amounts of power emanate from the floor below.

Emily.

It has to be Emily.

Another nightmare.

As soon as he opens his bedroom door, he hears her screaming.

Earlier in the day, she had caught her room on fire, so tonight she sleeps in a guest room, meaning he doesn't have as far to travel. He arrives at her room just seconds before Patrick.

Patrick doesn't hesitate to open the door. He smashes through, and Jerrick follows. Maggie stands guard next to the bed, barking at the intruders, while objects in the room rattle at the walls like they are trying to escape the energy pouring out of Emily. The bed snaps in two as her body levitates above the mattress. Her back arches further, and her shrill scream rings in their ears. Her eyes are closed, her face pale as fire burns across the ceiling.

Jerrick turns to Patrick, seeing his own fear mirrored in Patrick's expression.

Patrick shouts, "Can you grab her? She's going to hurt herself or one of us. I can't go in there when she's like this or she'll kill me."

Lathe arrives, halting in the doorway when he sees what's inside. It's a scene from the exorcist, reminiscent to one of his mother's episodes. But his mother didn't have fire sparking out of her.

"What the hell?" Lathe asks when Emily's skin begins to glow, setting fire to her clothes.

"Jerrick, do your thing," Patrick demands, running into the flaming room, and moving quickly to the bathroom.

Jerrick is from the Isa bloodline. His lineage gives him the ability to direct water. Usually, there has to be a direct source of water, which is why Patrick went to turn on the water. But Jerrick can focus his gifts so precisely that he is able to manipulate the water inside a person's body. Jerrick hates using this gift on people he cares about, and there aren't many people he cares about more than Emily.

"It's for her own safety," Lathe says.

Jerrick responds, "Can you do something about the wind?" It takes precision, and if he messes up, he could easily kill her.

Lathe stills the air in the room, and everything that was floating around the room's perimeter drops to the floor.

Jerrick senses Emily's pulse from across the room, the water in her body making her susceptible to his gifts. He steadies his nerves before matching his pulse to Emily's erratic heartbeat. Then he grabs hold of her just as Patrick comes out of the bathroom with a stream of water following him. He directs the water to Emily, drenching her to put out her burning clothes.

Jerrick hears Emily's screams inside his head as she mentally attacks him without mercy. Within a second, she uncovers his biggest weakness and uses it against him.

He tries to fight it, but his dead wife is standing in front of him. She is whole, beautiful, looking well, and happy. In her arms is their young son. His little arms reach out to Jerrick.

Jerrick knows this isn't possible, but it feels so real as he reaches out and takes his son in his arms. He squeezes him tight, hearing his little voice, and his wife moves forward, her hand touching his face. Her touch is tangible, soft and intimate. And his hold on Emily slips.

His wife's smile dies, and she says, "You killed our boy."

He swallows.

"You killed our son," she accuses again, her perfect healthy body turning into a rotting corpse.

"No," he chokes, clinging to the small body held tightly in his grip.

She drops her hand, accusing, "You're the reason we're dead. You killed us."

His son turns in his arms and asks, "Daddy, why did you let them kill me?"

Jerrick tries to blink away his tears, trying to focus on the family that is becoming less and less tangible. His son falls away from him into a pile of bones at his feet, his question haunting Jerrick.

PATRICK WATCHES Jerrick collapse like he no longer possesses the strength to stand. The giant of a man—usually unshakeable—falls apart, moaning and sobbing. His fist thumps against the floorboards as his inhuman cry fills the room.

The sound sends a chill through Patrick, and he realizes what Emily must have done. She's completely out of control. He never thought she would stoop to this level. And how is it possible? She's barely conscious.

Lathe shouts, "Patrick, what's happening?"

"She got in his head. Guard yourself, Lathe."

As he says the words, he feels her caress the inside of his psyche. "Paaaatrick," she coos inside his mind.

She is his greatest weakness, and he doesn't know how to stop her. The room fades away, and Patrick is standing on the balcony back in Connecticut. The ocean waves lap at the shore beneath him. Emily's soft touch on his arm has him spinning to face her. Her red flowing gown undulates in the cool breeze. Her hand strokes his jaw, and she lifts on her toes to place a tender kiss against his lips.

He knew she had a soft spot for him, their relationship more intimate than her and Jerrick. Her fingers caress behind his ear, and just before her lips meet his, she breathes, "You make it almost too easy, Patrick."

His concern dissipates as they kiss until a familiar male voice comes from behind him, sounding deceivingly cheerful. "Well, isn't this interesting."

Patrick's lips stop moving as fear crawls up his spine to muddle his thoughts. He pulls away from Emily as tears blur his vision, but not enough to miss the change in her expression. Her emerald eyes shine with a cruel glint, and her lips curl into a ruthless grin. His heart drops, his disbelief freezing him to the spot.

"Why?" Patrick pleads. "We are trying to help you, Emily."

Emily fades away, and he prays that's all, but Sky's voice comes again, and this time his hand materializes on Patrick's shoulder. "Patrick, I'm disappointed. I know I taught you better."

Patrick turns to face his nightmare. Sky looks to be in his early forties when really, he should have been dead over a century ago. His fine light hair brushes his thin shoulders. His silky black robe drapes open, leaving his pale chest exposed.

Sky wears a deceivingly friendly smile, but it doesn't reassure Patrick. Sky never wore his brutality on the outside. He left it to simmer below the surface. Patrick knew. He'd had more than a glimpse of the evil living beneath those sky-blue eyes.

Patrick shakes his head. "You aren't real. You're dead."

"Foolish boy, I will always live inside your memory. I'm unforgettable. We've shared too much, and our lives are forever intertwined." He lifts his hand to Patrick's face, but instead of a caress, his fingers grip Patrick's head, and he shoves him to the side, pushing with so much strength that Patrick falls onto the bed that appears out of nowhere.

Patrick crawls across it, trying to get away, but Sky is on him, tearing at his clothes before he can escape.

It isn't real. Part of him knows that, but Sky's touch feels so vivid. His voice is the same as it had been. He smells and tastes like he had before, and it breaks Patrick all over again. He tries to fade away like he used to, but he can't go numb because this nightmare won't let him escape.

After everything Patrick has been through, he thought he was strong enough to stand his own against the man who warped his mind and abused him so horribly, but the convoluted relationship still haunts him. In a twisted way, he loved Sky as much as he hated him, and his overall fear of the man drowns out his bravery. Emily gave Patrick the courage he needed to stand up to Sky, but she took it all away when she placed Patrick here with his worst nightmare.

LATHE WATCHES Patrick grip the wall like it's the only thing holding him up. Emily got to both men, and he's sure she is coming for him next. It's unnerving to see two of the strongest people he knows fall apart in a matter of seconds, but Lathe's whole life has been a nightmare, so what could she do to him. He feels her at the confines of his mind and knows he has to wake her. He has to put an end to this.

She is no longer screaming or levitating. Her drenched body, covered in burned clothes and soot, looks peaceful lying on the broken bed. How does he wake her?

He slaps her, but it doesn't seem to do anything but sting his palm and get Maggie to growl at him.

Think, think, think.

Something has to work.

Deja runs into the room, screaming, "Lathe, Ashley is petrifying! I need help getting her back to Latovia."

The timing is suspicious, so he asks, "When does the sun set?"

"The day after tomorrow," she says irritably, "Come on!"

He had her memorize passwords for this kind of occasion, and now he's glad he did. He follows her out of the room, looking back at Patrick and Jerrick, feeling bad he has to leave.

They make it down to the basement and take the new elevator Lathe installed, reaching the tunnel floor much faster than if they would have taken the crumbling steps.

As soon as the doors open, he bursts from it, searching for Ashley. He finds her quickly enough as she sits on the back of a twenty-foot-tall dragon.

"You could never be one of us!" Ashley shouts, and her dragon blows fire. Lathe dodges it, diving out of the way just in time. Deja is hiding behind a notch in the crumbling stone wall by the elevator.

"Deja, get upstairs. Go!" Lathe ushers her onto the elevator before turning to face Ashley.

Part of him doubts any of this is real. It can't be. Ashley wouldn't lie to him.

"Are you surprised, baby?" Ashley says, dismounting. "I just wanted to show you what she could do. I knew you'd get out of the way." She wears a smile that is so Ashley, and her walk is just like Ashley's walk. He's sure this has to be her, but the dragon doesn't fit. Neither does Deja. Deja looked scared. She seemed unsure, and for a moment, Lathe considers the idea that she led him into a trap.

Ashley is still walking toward him, saying, "They swore me to secrecy, but I want to tell you everything."

Deja comes out of nowhere, running up behind Ashley.

She's like a feline stalking prey, and before Lathe can react or Ashley can prepare, Deja jumps on her back and drives Lathe's sleek blade across Ashley's throat.

"No!" Lathe yells, running forward, but Deja moves away and shouts, "Now!"

The dragon engulfs Ashley's body in flames. Lathe pushes forward, the blaze searing his skin. The flames fade and Lathe falls to the ground next to Ashley's black charred remains.

"This isn't real," he tells himself, but his grief feels real. His anger is overwhelming. He looks up at Deja, his fury making him want to rip her apart, but Deja is like family to him.

"Why?" he asks her.

"Because she would tell you all of Latovia's secrets."

He shakes his head, "This isn't real."

Closing his eyes, he focuses on his breathing, trying to calm himself. He tries to focus on his other senses. There is the damp smell that he never could completely get rid of down here. The air is cool, but the floor is warm where the dragon had breathed fire. That can't be. Then he hears the big breaths of a monstrous creature. The smell of burning flesh overshadows the damp smell. The little girl in front of him feels real as she kneels in front of him.

"Lathe?" Deja says to him, trying to grab his attention.

"How could you, Deja?"

"How could I what?"

"I . . . " He stares at Ashley's body, refusing to believe it.

"She deserved to die!" Deja says, "Lathe, look at me."

Lathe looks up into Deja's anxious face as he asks, "Are you going to kill me next? Is this what things have come to?"

"Only if I have to," her mouth doesn't move with her words. And then her mouth opens, and she says, "Lathe, you're scaring me."

He spins around and sees Deja on his other side. There are two, but only one is real. Despite his confusion, he takes a breath of relief, knowing Ashley is safe. He grabs onto the Deja in front of him, the one who looks concerned. He hugs her, asking, "Deja, where is Ashley?"

The Deja he clings to says, "In Latovia, should I get her?" The other Deja tries to shout over her, "She's dead!"

"No, Deja, don't leave me," he pleads, "Keep talking. Keep talking to me."

BREAKING POINT

5

THE SUN COMES through the window at an angle, lighting up the room as Emily opens her eyes. She feels rested, something she hasn't felt in weeks. Maggie is lying across her chest. Her very bare chest. She sits up, crossing her arms over her breasts, finding herself sitting in a puddle on the broken mattress while her burned clothes fall from her in soaking tatters. The ceiling is charred, and the room a mess with books, pillows, and clothes strewn all over the place. And then she finds Patrick sitting on the floor by the window, his head resting against his steepled hands.

"P . . . " she croaks, then clears her throat, trying again, "Patrick?" He doesn't respond, and she wonders if he's asleep.

Movement in the hall catches her eye and she sees Jerrick pacing outside of her room. She almost calls to him, but hears him murmuring to himself, anxious mumblings she can't quite make out.

"What the hell happened here?" she asks Maggie, the

dog clinging to her side.

"You happened," Patrick says, his voice hard.

She spins to look at him. A ghostly tint diminishes his usual flawless sun-kissed complexion. His piercing blue eyes are bloodshot, and his dry lips pull into a tight frown, but it doesn't keep them from quivering.

She can't tell whether it's from fear or anger, but she can't sense a single emotion from him, which spreads a terrible chill of trepidation through her. It has been a long time since Patrick hid himself from her.

"What do you mean, I happened?"

His glare is cold, his voice callous. "You tell me, Emily."

She glances around the room, searching for answers, but her mind is blank.

"We tried to help you, and you—" He scrubs his face, a very uncharacteristic move. He stands, looks directly at her and says, "You tortured us, Emily."

He walks out without another word, and Jerrick doesn't stop his muttering as Patrick passes by.

What the hell had she done? She remembers nothing from the night before, but obviously something happened.

She's guessing the *us* Patrick mentioned involves Lathe and Jerrick, and she hopes they fared better than Patrick.

She gets out of bed, takes a quick shower, and throws on some clothes before leaving the room to search for Lathe. Jerrick comes to a standstill in the hall when Emily appears in at the doorway. His bloodshot eyes are wide as he says, "Vezetö."

"Jerrick, what happened?"

If pain has a face, it is the one Jerrick gives Emily before his mind seems to take him somewhere else. At his distant gaze, Emily steps around him, going toward Lathe's room. When she finds it empty, she checks the library before going downstairs. She tries to call out to him through a mental connection, but gets no response.

In this mansion, Lathe could hide from her indefinitely, but she prays he doesn't. She climbs down the basement steps just as the elevator to the tunnel below dings open.

She expects Lathe but is met by Deja instead. Deja charges out at her, shoving Emily against the opposite wall. The girl kicks at Emily's knee, knocking her down. Emily doesn't want to fight back, not against a child, but Deja knows how to handle herself.

Emily's mental manipulation doesn't work against the girl since she's Latovian, but her physical gifts work. She forces Deja back with a gust of wind, pinning her to the wall by the elevator.

Deja clenches her jaw, her nostrils flaring as her chest rises and falls in rapid succession. She tries to fight the air holding her back, but she can't, which only infuriates her more.

Emily gets to her feet, rubbing her knee. "Deja, what was that?"

Still held in place, Deja spits toward Emily.

Emily stares at the saliva on the floor between them before trying another question. "Where's Lathe?"

"I'll die before I tell you anything," she shouts.

"Deja!" Emily and Deja spin toward Lathe's voice. "Deja, I told you to stay in Latovia," he says, coming down the corridor toward them.

"Yeah, but—"

"Lathe!" Emily interrupts. "What happened? She's

attacking me, Jerrick's almost unresponsive, and Patrick can't even look at me without disgust."

Lathe nods toward Deja. "Let her go, and we can talk."

Emily lets go of the air holding Deja, and the girl lunges at her.

Lathe catches her mid-air, spins her around, and hits the button for the elevator. The doors slide open and he puts her on her feet. "Deja, I won't say it again. Go keep an eye on Ashley."

Deja looks angry but doesn't object as the doors close between them.

Lathe spins back to Emily. "She had every right to attack you. You made me watch her slit Ashley's throat last night before a dragon turned Ashley's body to ash. You made her say horrible things to me. You made me doubt her, and if it weren't for the real Deja being there to pull me out of it, I would've sunk deeper into the horrific nightmare you made me live last night."

Emily shakes her head, wanting to deny all of it. "I don't remember anything. I just woke up from the first real sleep I've had in weeks and everything is a disaster."

Lathe steps closer. "We woke in the middle of the night after feeling a torrent of power coming from your room. We came to check on you, and you were floating above your bed and burning your ceiling. We tried to put the fire out and wake you, but you dug into our brains and used our biggest fears against us. I don't know what the others went through, but I snapped out of it after only an hour because of Deja. When I went to check on Patrick and Jerrick, they were stuck in a dream state I couldn't break them out of."

Emily covers her face for a moment, taking a deep

breath. She runs a hand through her damp hair. "Lathe, I didn't know. I remember nothing from last night. I don't know how this happened."

"You've become unpredictable and dangerous, Emily. I put a notice out to the council, informing them we are undergoing renovations and will need to move our meetings to the Mahoney's estate. We need to fix whatever this is that's going on with you. If Jerrick and Patrick are awake, I'd like to go see them."

Emily steps back. "They wouldn't tell me anything. Hopefully, they will talk to you."

HOURS LATER, Lathe calls Emily into her own office. The office she hasn't been using lately due to her mental instability. Patrick stands by a bookshelf close to the door, avoiding her gaze, while Jerrick sits on the edge of a winged back chair in his workout gear, the damp stains showing he just came from a workout. His elbows rest on his thighs, and his forehead sits against a palm as he stares at the floor.

Lathe sits on the couch, looking the most relaxed. He pats the seat next to him.

As soon as Emily sits, Lathe cuts straight to the chase, "We moved a bed into the war room. We agreed you should sleep there tonight."

"It's a precaution, so you don't burn down the mansion," Jerrick adds.

Patrick says, "Or torture us some more."

She nods. "I understand." She swipes away a tear and looks to Patrick. "Do you mind if Maggie stays with you?"

He glares at her. "I think that's best."

Lathe shifts in his seat to face Emily. "Do you know how we can help you?"

She blinks away more tears before shaking her head. "No. No, I don't."

"But you said you slept well last night?" Lathe asks.

"Yeah, it's the first good night sleep I've had in months."

Patrick folds his arms over his chest and chuckles. "So, all you need is to torture people in your sleep, and you'll feel rested."

"Patrick, please . . . " Her voice catches and she stops talking.

"Please, what, Emily? Let you torture us some more?"

"I don't know what happened. I don't remember anything. I didn't mean for . . . any of this."

"It's okay, Emily." Jerrick gives her a reassuring look. "We'll figure this out."

"It's not okay!" Patrick shouts.

She lets out a heavy breath and glares up at him while her jaw hardens. "You know I didn't mean to hurt anyone, Patrick, least of all, you. I'm trying to make this better, and your jabs aren't helping."

"She's right," Lathe says.

With a clenched jaw, Patrick pins Emily with a glare. "I'm sorry I'm not making this easy enough on you. Next time you torture us, I'll try to be more considerate of *your* feelings."

"Now you're just being an asshole for sport," she says, standing from the couch.

He steps towards her. "*You* don't get it."

She stares back, standing her ground, until he shakes his

head and turns, moving toward the door. A sudden gust of wind comes from Emily, slamming the door before Patrick reaches it. He spins to her.

She steps forward, saying, "You stay. I'll leave so you guys can discuss me behind my back while I go put myself in solitary."

"How like you to pity yourself in this moment," Patrick sneers.

The tears betray her even as she laughs. "And how disappointing that you go back to acting like the old Patrick after one night with your past."

"One night with my past?" his voice vibrates with rage as he stalks toward her. "Since we're sugar coating shit, try not to think about the real reason we're putting you in the war room. It's the only remaining defense we have against you, but we'll only drown you if you force our hand."

She crosses her arms. "Force your hand! When have I ever forced you to do anything, Patrick? It's not my fault that you're always the first to offer yourself up. Honestly, I'm surprised you didn't enjoy a night with Sky. I mean, how many times have I tortured you? I thought sadism was just your thing."

He leans down, so his face is only inches from hers. "You, Emily. You were my thing. I let *you* torture me, and I dealt with it because it was *you*. But last night. That wasn't you! You've been in my head. You know what he did to me! He destroyed me, and then I met you, and you gave me hope." He straightens his spine and steps back, shaking his head. "But last night, you took it away when you made me helpless."

Emily swallows, stepping forward, she reaches for him,

her voice softer, "Patrick—"

He steps out of her reach, looking at her hand like it's diseased. Making eye contact, he says, "You've ruined this." He waves a hand between them. "Us. I can't even look at you without—" he shakes his head, unwilling to give his feelings a name. He starts again, "Maybe I'm hurting your feelings by blaming you, but you destroyed us, Emily."

She swallows, barely holding onto her composure, but Patrick isn't finished. He looks around the room. "I mean, how close are any of us?" He points to Jerrick. "Jerrick's twisted loyalty to you is based on you murdering the man that murdered his wife and little boy. You and Lathe were sired by the same evil man that neither of you wants to claim, so why are you pretending that you're suddenly siblings when you barely know each other?" He throws his arms out. "And in case you forgot, I killed Lathe's girlfriend. I may as well have killed Jerrick's family. I did nothing to prevent it." He looks at Jerrick and shakes his head. "That will always haunt me, but not like it haunts you."

"Enough!" Lathe stands from the couch.

Patrick laughs without humor. "It is enough. We're all murderers. I guess it makes sense, Olvasho kill their way to the top, don't we?"

"I haven't killed anyone," Emily whispers.

"Really?" Patrick narrows his eyes. "For fuck's sake, Emily. I'm done sparing your feelings. Just because you didn't mean to kill anyone, doesn't make you any less of a killer. Your sheer power alone slaughtered the men in the compound the night Sky died. And you can phrase it differently if it makes you feel better, but you also killed Sky. He had to die. It was the only way he'd stop torturing and massacring everyone. So stop with this 'I freed the souls, and he died bullshit.' You are the reason the monster is dead. Mostly dead, anyway." He taps his forehead. "He is still very much alive up here."

He continues, looking at Emily, "So, I guess what I'm saying is I hope Jerrick will drown you if that's what it comes to, but I won't. I can't because as much as I hate you right now, I love you more, and dear God, I can't afford to love you anymore. I can't do any of this anymore. With Sky, at least I could anticipate the torture. With you, I never know what comes next. I certainly didn't expect your malice to contend with your father's. But this time I can walk away, so I am. I'm out. I'm sure the rest of the Olvasho will be thrilled." He takes a step toward the door before adding, "I'm taking Maggie with me because she deserves a break from your torture, too."

He turns the doorknob and walks out of the office, leaving a troublesome silence in his wake.

Emily stares out after him, cut to the quick. When she blinks, tears fall.

Jerrick is the first to break the silence, saying, "He tried to stop it. He tried to keep my family safe. Sky punished him for it, but he did try. And almost died for it."

"I don't blame you guys if you want out," Emily says, unable to look at them.

Lathe leans back on the sofa and props his legs up on the ottoman. "This is my home. I'm not leaving."

Emily looks at Jerrick, who is staring at the floor. He confesses, "I need to be here. It's the only thing that gives me purpose." He swallows. "It's the only thing that's keeping me alive."

SURPRISE VISITOR

6

Morgan and Alec are snuggling on the couch when there is a knock at the apartment door. Morgan pulls away from Alec to sit up straight. "Who's here at ten-thirty?"

A second later, the lock disengages, and the door opens. Alec stands, putting himself between Morgan and the door, but relaxes as he watches Patrick walk in with Maggie at his heel.

Morgan jumps up and rounds Alec. "Patrick, what are you doing here?"

Patrick sets a duffle bag on the dining table and looks between Morgan and Alec as Maggie moves forward to say *hello*.

Morgan supplies, "Alec just stopped by for help with a problem he was having, but he was just about to leave." She bends down to pet Maggie.

Alec gives her a look before closing his eyes and shaking his head.

Patrick leans against the table and says, "I don't want to be a groomsman."

"What?" Morgan asks.

Alec sits on the arm of the couch. "Morgan, you are the worst liar. I came here with a problem? Shit," he says through a chuckle. "Not to mention, he reads minds."

"He doesn't read my mind," she defends. "He promised."

Alec pulls her back to his chest and kisses her cheek. "You're fucking adorable."

"And hopeless," Patrick adds.

Morgan scowls. "What are you doing here, Patrick?"

"It's still my apartment. I do still have a room here, right?"

"Of course, but why are you here?"

Patrick lets out a long sigh before saying, "Emily tortured us all night while she slept. Right now, Lathe and Jerrick have her locked in the war room and I . . . I just quit, so now I'm here."

Morgan takes a step toward him. "What do you mean you quit?"

Alec says, "What do you mean she tortured you?"

Patrick walks into the open kitchen and gets into the cabinet next to the fridge, pulling out a bottle of bourbon and a glass. He pours himself half a glass, downing it before turning back toward Morgan and Alec, offering, "Would either of you like some?"

Morgan shakes her head, but Alec steps forward. "I can't let you drink alone, man."

Patrick nods and turns around to fill another glass for Alec. As he hands it to him, Morgan says, "She tortured you?"

"Not just me. She made Lathe watched Deja kill Ashley. Jerrick's dead wife and son visited him and asked why he let them die. And I got to spend my night with Sky."

Morgan sucks in a breath. Patrick had gotten into the habit of letting down his guard with Morgan, but with Alec here, Morgan didn't expect Patrick to expose so much.

Patrick pours himself another drink and walks into the living room, taking the chair next to the couch. Maggie settles at his feet.

Morgan looks at Alec, who mouths, "Should I go?"

Morgan shrugs.

"Don't go on my account," Patrick says without looking in their direction. "Maggie and I will stay out of your way."

Morgan joins Patrick in the living room, sitting at the end of the couch to face him. "I don't want you to stay out of the way. I want you to explain what you mean when you say you quit."

He strokes Maggie's head with his free hand. "The details would hurt you."

"I'm not as fragile as you sometimes think."

Alec joins Morgan on the couch. Sipping his drink before commenting, "Sounds like he doesn't want to talk about it right now."

Morgan sighs, then asks, "What is Maggie doing here with you?"

"I'll take her back when it's safe."

Morgan scowls, unsatisfied with his answer. Before she continues probing, Alec lays his hand on her arm. When she looks at him, he shakes his head, pleading with her to stop asking questions.

"Okay, fine. You guys can keep each other entertained. I have to shower anyway."

She walks down the hall to her room.

After a beat of silence, Patrick asks, "Why don't you hate me?"

"Why would I hate you?" Alec asks.

"Because of Ben and because most people do."

"Ben doesn't hate you, man. Besides, I know what you've done to save him and to protect Emily. Is the War room, the concrete gymnasium where you all fought each other, and I had to carry that huge ass rock?"

"Yeah."

After a lull, Alec says, "I thought you loved her."

"I do."

"But you gave up."

Patrick stares into his drink as he answers, "My previous sadistic relationship conditioned me to accept abuse and call it love. I barely survived. Emily forcing me to spend a night with my worst fear showed me I was dangerously close to being right back in the same situation. I had to leave. Not because I *don't* love her, but because I do."

"Good for you for leaving."

"It doesn't feel good."

"The right decisions rarely do."

Patrick glances at him. "You've changed."

"Yeah, no thanks to you fucking with my brain."

"I could've just killed you."

Alec snickers. "What, and ruin your relationship with Morgan? Never."

"You don't know—"

"Yeah, I do, because you could've gone anywhere, but

you came here. Morgan is your safe place. She's one of the few people who stands up to you and calls you on your bull-shit, and when you realize she's right, she'll hold you together and build you back up because she's fucking amazing."

"And what about you?" Patrick asks, before going on to answer, "I can tell you want to be good enough for her, but you're not."

Alec laughs, "Fuck you, man. I already know that, but she thinks I'm good enough for her, and that's all that really matters."

"I suppose you're right, but I still feel a duty to threaten you."

Alec raises an eyebrow. "If I hurt her, I'll save you the trouble and castrate myself."

Patrick smirks. "How noble of you."

REPERCUSSIONS

7

EMILY PRAYS Lathe and Jerrick hadn't abandoned her too. She sits shivering on the cement floor in the middle of the War room, waiting for someone to let her out. With bent knees, her naked thighs press against her bare chest. Her teeth chatter as she rubs her palms over her exposed skin. She blinks and moisture drips from her lashes. She lets it fall, no longer making an effort to wipe away tears. They had become one with the water a while ago, and now she's not even sure if she's still crying.

Scraps of a sheet lay in tatters across her shoulders, while her wet hair clings to her skin, dripping silent paths down her back and collecting on the concrete floor. She is numb with fear, yet full of shame. She woke up to find her bed torn to shreds, and what remains of her clothes are ash.

The paralyzing panic comes in waves. What if they had left her here? What if there was no way out? What if she killed them in her sleep and doesn't remember it?

Her anxiety rises, and power pours out of her in nervous waves, causing bed shards to rattle against the walls.

She reins it in when she hears the door's lock release with a clunk. She wants to stand, but her legs are shaky, and she would be completely exposing her nakedness.

The door swings open, and Lathe appears. Without a word, he approaches and drapes a fluffy pink robe over her shoulders.

She clings to it, wrapping it tighter. "Did I hurt anyone?"

"Only yourself."

"I'm fine," she says through chattering teeth.

"You tried to burn your way out of here, which is why you're wet. It seems your body is somewhat flame retardant, at least to your own flames. We're working on having some flame-resistant clothing made."

As she gets to her feet, she looks to the ceiling where the remnants of a camera are dangling. "Did you get footage?"

"Some."

She starts walking toward the exit. "I want to see it."

Lathe follows her out of the concrete gymnasium, and into the guest room that they converted into a control room. They had set up a few monitors, and Lathe goes straight to the computer to push play.

Emily watches herself on the screen.

"I'll fast forward to where you fell asleep." He does so, and presses play.

On the screen, a sleeping Emily levitates off her bed, the blankets hang over her body as she ascends. At first, she just hangs in the air, but soon the bed vibrates. The vibration increases until the whole thing is rattling against the floor.

Emily's hair swirls, and the blanket and sheet are

whisked off of her, flying in opposite directions. Next, the wood bed frame shatters. Its splinters fly around like shrapnel. Then the mattress explodes. Its soft insides soar around the room in an irregular haphazard pattern, ricocheting off the walls and ceiling.

And through all the commotion, Emily hovers, untouched by the chaos. Soon her arms float out beside her, her palms up. Her eyes open, giving her a creepy air. Flames burst from her palms, and the current bouncing around the room catches fire, leaving flaming bits of foam and wood, reverberating off the walls. Emily lowers to her feet, landing softly on the cement while her palms lift into the air, shooting flames up to the gymnasium's high ceiling. Once there is a cloud of fire, she lowers her arms and allows the blaze to fall, dripping from the ceiling like fizzling fireworks. The flames don't seem to bother her skin or hair, but her clothes catch fire.

The sprinklers come on, dousing the fire in a matter of seconds, but Emily appears agitated by the moisture. She walks the perimeter of the room like a caged animal looking for a way out. When she can't find one, she walks to the hidden door, and at close range, blasts it with white-hot flames.

The sprinklers turn off, and Emily steps back from the door, lowering her arms. She scopes the ceiling and spots the video camera. She takes a running leap, and the air carries her up to the ceiling, where she melts through the protective glass bubble around the video camera. She reaches in, grabbing the camera. It captures a closeup of her dilated black eyes just before the picture scrambles and goes black.

Emily rewinds a few seconds and pauses on her closeup face. The face of a stranger.

Eventually, Lathe says, "There's more."

She looks up at him. "What do you mean?"

"This is also from last night." He flips to another surveillance feed, this one of the control room. On-screen, Jerrick and Lathe are staring at the computer monitor. Emily didn't know they added surveillance in this room.

"She's going to set herself on fire," Lathe says on screen.

"Turning on the sprinkler system," Jerrick says, typing something into the computer.

Lathe watches the screen. "That pissed her off."

"She can't get through that door," Jerrick reassures.

Everything in the control room begins to shake.

Lathe says, "You sure about that?"

"These walls are four feet thick."

Lathe waves an arm. "Yet, she's moving everything in here."

Jerrick types something else into the computer. "Turning them off." Everything in the room goes still.

"I guess we just let her catch herself on fire then. It seems she'd rather burn than get wet."

Lathe turns off the monitor, and Emily sits back in her chair. "I have no memory of anything. What else did I do?"

"Not much. You wandered around the room, caught things on fire, and propelled things around. You didn't seem to know what you were doing, but you got mad every time we turned on the water."

"Was I naked the whole time?"

Lathe lets out a breath. "Yes, for most of it. We weren't

focusing on your body. We were more interested in what you were doing."

She buries her face in her hands. "Why is this happening?"

He shrugs. "Wish I knew."

She wishes Patrick were here. He would hug her and reassure her everything would be all right. She needs him to lie to her and tell her everything would work out. But Patrick left, maybe because he finally realized nothing would be okay, and he was done lying.

Lathe rests a hand on her shoulder, causing her to jump. He pulls away. "Sorry, just trying to be—"

"It's okay. You don't need to do that." She stands. "Thank you, Lathe. For everything." She moves toward the door. "I'm going to go take a shower."

She leaves the room, and Lathe goes back to the footage.

ASHLEY ENTERS WOLFE's throne room, unsure why it's still called a throne room since Wolfe had switched the throne for a desk years ago. The guards don't even check to see if it's okay with Wolfe before she barges in. She suspects it's because they're frightened of her. Ashley knows they still give Deja a hard time, and Wolfe has known her a lot longer.

Wolfe looks up from his desk as the heavy wooden door bangs closed behind her. The room is yet another cave with high ceilings and gemstones glittering across its concave dome.

She cuts straight to the point. "Wolfe, I know I've asked

you before, but you aren't hiding dragons somewhere, are you?"

He drops his head and goes back to work on the map in front of him. It's a map of the caves. A narrow passage recently collapsed. Though no one was hurt, it has been making everyone antsy.

He moves a ruler around the map. "Everyone in Latovia doubts me, and now you are too?"

Ashley steps forward. "What are you doing?"

"Trying to follow the fault lines to see if we should expect another cave-in."

"You can predict that kind of thing?"

"I don't know. It's never happened before. The magic inside Latovia has protected us, but the magic is waning. The caves are fragile. I'm not sure we can count on magic alone to keep us safe.

Ashley notices the Seismology textbooks lying next to the giant map. "So, you're learning about earthquakes?"

"And other earth vibrations."

"So you have your hands full. Can I help?"

Wolfe peeks at her. "How are you with science?"

"I mean, I've always been an A student, but I'm not sure how much of this I can help with. I wish we had the internet down here."

"Even if we did, the technology to use it wouldn't work. The magic effects it."

Ashley pulls the book in front of her and begins reading. "This is actually kind of interesting."

She continues to read for the next half hour, only stopping when Wolfe places his hand on the page she's reading.

She looks up, but Wolfe isn't looking at her. He's staring

at the ceiling where the gems are shimmering as they vibrate. "Do you feel that?" he asks.

"Do you think it's an earthquake?"

"It could be another piece of Latovia collapsing."

"You know what else makes vibrations?" Ashley says, "Big dragons."

Without looking up, he says, "You think I have a secret stash of dragons stowed away somewhere?"

Ashley bites her lip and shrugs.

Wolfe faces her slowly. "No, Ashley. The dragons are all dead. They died out during your father's reign."

"Eww, don't call him that."

"Sorry, King Mazilon," he corrects.

"So how do you explain my visions?"

"I don't. I have no idea what you're seeing, but instead of worrying about the non-existent dragons you're seeing, my priority is freeing our people. Evelyn gave us more time, but if we don't come up with another solution, we'll be out of magic in the next few months."

"I've been working on my magic. I might be able to do what Evelyn did on a smaller scale."

Deja slips in the door. "Wolfe, some orphans witnessed a summoning."

Wolfe stands and looks to Ashley, "You should come and see what happens when the Latovian people break the law. This type of magic is forbidden for a reason." He grabs his weapon belt and his long dragon skin jacket before walking out with Deja in the lead.

Once they pass the guards, Deja turns, walking backward, to warn, "It's nasty."

Ashley follows them, saying, "I thought I was the only one who had working magic."

Wolfe shakes his head. "Sorry to pop your balloon, princess. Every Latovian carries a small spark, and when enough gather with the intent to create something, things usually become unpredictable and dangerous."

"First, it's pop your bubble, and second, dangerous how?"

Wolfe glances at her. "You'll see."

Ashley takes in his jacket, realizing this isn't the one he usually wears. "Were all the dragons black?"

"None of them were black." His head tilts to the side as his eyes narrow on her. "Did you think we skinned our dragons?"

His look makes Ashley uneasy. "Is there another way?"

"The dragons shed their scales like a snake," he explains. "Just before molting, their skin and scales turned black. Once they shed their skin, their new scales would be vibrant colors, but the skin they left behind was thick and warm like leather, only nothing had to die."

"So, you guys didn't kill the dragons for their skin?"

Deja snorts, saying, "That's like asking if you would skin your golden retriever for its coat."

"Dragons were more than just part of our family," Wolfe explains, "They were living deities to the Latovian people. They encompassed Latovia's power. They were part of its essence, and without them, Latovia has not been the same." He turns, asking, "Deja, where were they spotted?"

"By the kilns." She leads them down a path.

Ashley rubs her arms, trying to warm herself. She didn't

think she would ever get used to the cold. "Does this happen often?"

Wolfe's fists clench as he grinds out, "It happens more than it used to. People are getting desperate."

"And Emily was supposed to help us, but she's a fucking mess," Deja adds.

Ashley can't help her smile at Deja's choice of words. The curse words just seem so out of place coming from the little girl. But the topic deserved the curse word because Emily really was a fucking mess from what Lathe and Deja had told her. That melts the smile from her face.

"We need to find a way to help them so they can help us," Wolfe says.

"It sounds like they don't know how to help her."

"Well, they need to figure it out. We don't have time to wait, princess. I know Emily is your friend, but right now, her instability is putting all of us at risk. And if Emily is too distracted to break the curse, we're all dead. We need to fix it, even if it's temporary."

"Temporary? She's been through enough, Wolfe. What she needs is real help, not a temporary fix."

"We all have demons. She needs to suck it up and deal."

Ashley's brows draw together, and she stops walking. "You're unbelievable."

Wolfe throws a glance over his shoulder as he continues forward. "I'm realistic. If I took the time to dissect every one of my feelings, my leadership would be called into question too."

Her legs carry her forward, pissed. "Are you kidding me! You think she's just being overly sensitive? She tortured them in her sleep, Wolfe!"

"But was she really even sleeping? Or is that what she wants them to think?"

"What could she possibly gain from torturing her friends?"

"Are they friends?"

"You're so cynical. The Olvasho care about one another. They care about Emily. They don't fight to the death in order to take leadership."

With gruff laughter, he says, "Oh yes, they do. It's just that they manipulate you while they do it, so you don't know who holds the power until someone slips up."

"You're a dick!"

Before the words are out of her mouth, he spins on her, shoving her against the cave wall. With his face inches from hers, he says, "I'm still your king!"

"You're not my king, and this is not my home."

Deja looks around nervously, but there are no other witnesses.

Wolfe pulls back. "I'm planning to meet with the Olvasho leaders during the new moon to persuade them to fix this." His dark eyes soften. "We're on the same side, Ashley, but things will only get worse. I know my people, and what we're about to see is only the beginning. The more desperate people become, the more reckless they'll be. Latovia will erupt into chaos. I'm a king. People depend on me to make the tough decisions that no one else wants to make, and so I do, every day. I am not heartless, but my first priority will always be to my people."

He nods to a nervous Deja, and she turns and continues showing the way.

Ashley moves forward reluctantly. She gets a sick feeling

the further they go, sensing the twisted, ugly feel of magic gone wrong.

They round a corner and go down another tunnel before hearing the commotion. A few people run past them, trying to flee the nasty magic.

The scene comes into view and has Ashley holding in a gasp. The blood drains from her face and tears prick in her eyes.

A girl, no older than fourteen, stands with a blood-spattered face, screaming at the sight in front of her. A middle-aged man is on the ground crying over a distorted body, while a woman around the same age stands in shock, looking down at her twisted, warped arm.

Against the stone wall behind the chaos is the crude outline of a door, shimmering with magically charged blood. Beneath it, two mangled bodies shrivel on the ground, their features so misshapen, they can no longer be identified.

Shocked by the horrifying scene, Ashley doesn't even realize she's stopped moving until Wolfe leans in next to her, whispering, "And this, kids, is why we don't play with magic."

Then, as if unfazed, he steps forward to quiet the screaming teen.

Deja steps closer to Ashley. "This is happening more frequently."

Ashley observes the eight-year-old by her side. Deja looks sad, but not at all traumatized.

"You shouldn't witness this," Ashley says, trying to block her view by stepping in the way.

"Please, this is nothing I haven't seen before," she says, rounding Ashley to go help Wolfe.

Feeling like a wuss, Ashley moves ahead, trying to comfort the woman with the twisted arm. Ashley tries to reverse the magic but cannot.

"Does it hurt?" she asks.

The woman shakes her head woodenly, her voice emotionless. "I don't feel it at all."

"Wolfe," Ashley calls. "I can't fix it, but it doesn't hurt her. What do we do?"

Wolfe steps forward, kneeling on the floor next to them. Wolfe takes the woman's mangled hand, inspecting it like it's nothing more than a twisted branch. Finally, he says, "Close your eyes."

She does as her king tells her, and Wolfe pulls her arm straight out. Before Ashley can react, he pulls a blade from his hip and slices through the woman's arm, just above the elbow.

TWISTED MINDS

8

Patrick flips a pancake in the skillet while Morgan works on her laptop at the kitchen bar.

As she closes her computer, she says, "Are you sure you don't want to go with me to the coffee shop tonight? You haven't seen Ben play with the rest of his group."

"Morgan, I'm not going."

"I hate leaving you behind."

"I'm a big boy. I'll be fine," he says, attempting to flip the next pancake, but the batter runs off the spatula. "This goo won't cook right."

Morgan tries to peek over Patrick's shoulder. "Let me see."

He turns around with the skillet in hand to show her.

With a grimace, Morgan says, "The consistency is off. The batter is too runny."

Patrick lifts a solid pancake. "This one made it."

Morgan makes a face. "It's black!"

"Are you discriminating against my pancakes?"

"You charred it. I didn't know that was possible."

"I quit," Patrick says, walking the skillet to the trash and dumping the gooey batter. "You said pancakes were foolproof."

She wrinkles her nose. "I thought they were."

He presses his lips together, looking at the mess he made in an attempt to be domestic. With a shrug, he abandons the mess and takes a seat at the bar next to Morgan.

"I'm not good at normal things."

"Because you can't make pancakes? That's okay. We'll order something."

"It's not just the pancakes. I don't know how to live a regular life. I can't even picture it."

"Things will get easier. Give it time. You grew accustomed to living in an extremely stressful environment. It will take time to adjust. I'm sure you have post-traumatic stress from everything you've been through."

His elbow rests against the counter, and he props his chin on his fist, frowning at the kitchen cabinets.

Morgan tilts her head as she stares at him. "What is it?"

After a deep inhale, he sighs. "Morgan, your attack in Florida, does it affect your personal life? Do you have trouble . . . Do you and Alec . . ." He exhales, starting again, "You guys seem so comfortable with one another."

She watches him for a moment before admitting, "I once flipped Preston off the couch for coming on to me. I felt pinned and reacted before I could process what was happening. I guess learning how to be with him has made it easier with Alec. I mean, I haven't freaked out on him, but I've also known Alec for a long time and already felt safe with him."

Patrick shakes his head, but his eyes don't meet hers. "I thought I was over my past with Sky, but Emily showed me how wrong I was and how weak I still am."

Her brows pull together and she keeps her voice soft, "I was assaulted and nearly raped. It was horrible, and it changed me. But it doesn't get to ruin my life, just like Sky doesn't get to ruin yours. I'm not downplaying what happened to you. I know that our experiences are vastly different, and you've endured a lot more trauma than I ever have. Have you talked to anyone about it?"

"No. Emily has seen some of it in my mind, and I'm sure Lathe and Jerrick know more than I'd like."

"But, you've never talked about it?"

"Only to you."

"Then talk to me, Patrick." She reaches out, laying her hand on his. "If you were anyone else, I would tell you to go for counseling, but I know that's not really safe for you. So, talk to me."

"I won't put that darkness on your shoulders. You're the only person who looks at me like I can be redeemed."

"I can't promise I won't get emotional, but I don't need you to protect me from the truth. I know the world can be a dark place, but it's a lot darker when you shut everyone out. What you tell me may hurt, but it's only because I hurt for you. That's what happens when you love someone. Their pain becomes your own. What you tell me won't change the way I love you."

"I don't want you to know."

"I'm asking you to trust me. Let someone else help carry your burdens."

He lets out a shaky breath, and his face falls into his

palm. "He twisted my mind, Morgan." He lifts his head. "He manipulated me into stabbing my mother to death. She was crying." His chin trembles. "And even as she knew she would die, she looked at me with affection." His voice breaks, and he covers his mouth like he can stifle the noise. He takes a breath before continuing, "She forgave me for killing her even though I didn't deserve it. Even if I didn't know what I was doing, I killed her by letting him manipulate me."

"I don't think that's your fault."

"She didn't want me to blame myself, but I could've done more to stop it. I should've done more to stop all of it, but I didn't know how, and after my mom died, I just wanted out, but he wouldn't let me die. The first time he raped me, I fought him, but I was no match. Eventually, I stopped fighting. I remember the day that I accepted my fate. The less defiance he felt from me, the kinder he was. I knew I couldn't escape him, so I found myself going out of my way to try to please him. I relied on him for everything. I worshipped and despised him. He made himself my entire world."

Morgan lays a hand on his arm. "The psychological abuse and manipulation you endured is awful and wrong. It's not your fault. None of it is your fault, Patrick, and you can get past this. I've seen how far you've come in a year. The person you are today isn't the same person you were then."

He shakes his head. "I'm the same person. I've just learned to bury the past until Emily pulled it out of me. How fucked up is it that I'm in love with the daughter of the man who sexually abused me for years? It's something I go out of my way to avoid thinking or talking about. I'd rather it never be brought up again, but when Isa was with me, she reopened those festering wounds. She helped me face some of it, but I never wanted it to control the way I live my life."

"Patrick, what did you want before Sky?"

"What do you mean?"

"I mean, what were your ambitions, your goals, your dreams? You must have wanted something."

"I wanted a home. My mom and I were already on the run by the time I turned six. We never spent more than a few months in one place. I hated it."

"You have a home here, Patrick. You are no longer on the run." She scoots back on her stool. "Hold on. I have to grab something." She hops up and hurries to her bedroom, returning a moment later with a notepad in her hand. She takes her seat next to Patrick.

Fiddling with the notepad, she looks him in the eye, saying, "I looked up a few things after some of the stuff you told me back when we were searching for Emily. I wrote down what I wanted to say to you, but it never seemed like the right time." She opens the notebook and begins reading. "Stop trying to make sense of the abuse because it doesn't make sense. You were forced to understand a world through Sky's distorted perspective, so of course you're confused. But what Sky did to you was wrong. You never deserved it. Don't waste your energy on your guilt, fear, and shame. What matters is you made it through. You're free. You survived. You can do anything now. So, first, forgive yourself."

Patrick's eyes glisten, and he opens his mouth to speak, but the knock on the front door has him closing his mouth and sitting straighter. His face becomes a blank slate, soon replaced with a pleasant smile that Morgan would swear was real under any other circumstance. "Were we expecting Alec?"

With regret, Morgan says, "When you announced you were cooking, I asked him to bring a pizza as a backup."

Patrick nods, looking unphased as he stands to get the door, but stops short when the door opens and Alec comes in. "Hey, it's me."

Patrick looks at Morgan. "He has a key?"

Morgan sits on her stool, barely able to hold in her tears as she nods, feeling like she let him down and worried he wouldn't open up to her again.

"I'll be in my room," Patrick says, walking away.

Alec sets the pizza on the counter. "There's enough for all of us."

His offer is met with the sound of Patrick's door closing. "Should I be offended?" Alec asks, looking to Morgan. "Hey, what's wrong?" He moves to stand in front of her.

She closes the notebooks in her hand. "Hold on, Alec. I'll be right back."

She walks after Patrick, knocking at his door before opening it. She finds him standing in the middle of the room, his head cocked, and brows raised in question. Without a word, she meets him in the middle of the room and hugs him. And after a few seconds of hesitation, he returns her hug. When he does, she says, "I feel like I let you down by inviting Alec."

"Morgan, you've never let me down."

She pulls back and hands him the notebook. "Maybe it'd

be helpful for you to write your feelings and thoughts. I wrote down some online support groups in there too."

He takes the notebook, saying, "So you've been holding on to this since last Fall?"

She shrugs. "Maybe."

He gives her a warm smile. "I'm lucky to have you, Morgan."

She smirks. "And don't forget it."

THE NEXT MORNING Patrick takes Maggie for a walk, and when he returns, he finds a note on his bed. He picks it up, finding a list of counselors.

He walks across the hall, knocking at Morgan's door.

"Come in."

He opens the door and finds her lying in bed with a book.

"What's this?" He holds up the paper.

She sits up straighter, saying, "I'm always happy to listen to you and try to help, but I think you might be in better hands with one of them. As long as you don't bring up Olvasho powers, they can treat your case like any other, and they're the professionals."

Alec enters the room from the bathroom, saying, "Hey, Patrick." Patrick scowls at him and takes a step forward as Alec sits on the bed next to Morgan.

Morgan says, "Patrick, why are you looking at him like you're about to suck his soul from his body?"

Alec, not realizing Patrick's glare, looks at him.

Patrick takes another step forward, intent on Alec. "Why can't I sense you?"

Alec shrugs.

Morgan says, "Jerrick said something similar."

"Something is going on with you," Patrick says to Alec. "Last night, I thought it was because I was distracted, but you've gone full shadow today, like a Latovian."

"He can't be Latovian," Morgan notes.

"I know, but it is curious. Can I peek at your mind?"

Alec frowns. "I don't like the sound of that."

"I'm trying to be polite," Patrick says.

"Meaning you're gonna do it either way?" Alec asks.

Patrick shrugs. "I'd rather you be willing."

"You're not gonna fuck with my head like last time, are you?"

"No."

"Go ahead."

Morgan moves closer to him, grabbing his hand as Patrick approaches the side of the bed. He touches Alec's temples and quickly pulls back like he's been zapped.

Patrick shakes his head as he backs up, his eyes wide. "I don't understand."

Morgan asks, "What is it?"

"There's nothing."

Morgan looks scared while Alec laughs, "Is this your twisted attempt at a joke?"

"No. I really don't sense anything. No memories, no thoughts. I don't understand."

Patrick suddenly winces, making a sound of protest and ducking as he cradles his head. Morgan hops off the bed and crouches next to him, but he soon recovers.

"What was that?" she asks when he regains his composure.

He stares at Alec, saying, "I couldn't sense you at all, and then something snapped, and all your thoughts bombarded my mind all at once.

"What does this mean?" Morgan asks.

Patrick shakes his head. "I have no idea."

TRAUMA

9

THEY STOPPED MOVING beds into the war room because they only get destroyed. Emily lies on a mat on the floor with a pillow and a blanket. Lathe and Jerrick watch Emily on the monitor and know she's fallen asleep when she floats off the floor in her silver flame resistant romper. Her blanket flies one direction while her mat rips in half, the two halves going opposite ways while her pillow explodes, the fluff bursting into flame as it, too, flies across the room.

Jerrick tilts his head toward Lathe. "I don't think this is a good idea, and we don't know how well that material will hold up."

"Shut up. It's the best choice we have," Ashley quips, standing in front of the door to the War room, waiting for them to open it for her.

Lathe shrugs. "I promised her."

Jerrick groans, "There is no way Wolfe is excited about this."

"I'm not," the gruff voice comes from behind them.

"Jesus," Lathe breathes, grabbing his chest.

A sly grin takes Wolfe's face. "You guys are so easy to sneak up on."

While Lathe glares at him, Jerrick says, "You have an unfair advantage. Maybe Lathe should put an alarm on the portal door."

"Or we could just make him wear a bell," Lathe suggests.

Wolfe grins. "Try. I dare you."

Tired of waiting on them, Ashley types in the code next to the door and the war room opens, drawing everyone's attention.

As she enters, she hears Lathe. "Shit, the whole place is on fire."

The sprinklers come on, and Jerrick warns, "The sprinklers will make her angry."

"It's already doused the fire. I'll turn them off."

The sprinklers cut off as the door latches behind Ashley. Her hooded jacket, pants, and boots are made from black dragon skin. When she suggested a tighter fit so she could look more like Catwoman, Wolfe shook his head and told her it was for function, not style, pointing out if it were tighter, she wouldn't be able to bend or move.

She pulls back her hood, and her blond hair gleams in the light. "Emily?" she calls.

Emily's eyes are closed, her breathing slow as she sleeps. The fact that she is levitating five feet off the floor gives Ashley the creeps. She walks towards her, trying to keep herself from fidgeting with the ring on her finger as she approaches Emily. She feels a niggling at the confines of her mind, but her Latovian blood keeps Emily from being able to control her.

"Emily?" she asks again, hoping to get through to Emily before Wolfe tries to pull something shady.

Ashley takes a step back when she feels Emily pull away mentally. And she jumps back as Emily burst into flames, the fire coming from every pore.

The sprinklers start again, and Ashley flips up her hood, backing further. Fire strikes out like a whip, and just before it smashes into Ashley, the flames slam into a shield of iridescent purple light that seemed to pop out of nowhere.

BACK IN THE CONTROL ROOM, Lathe gasps, looking to Wolfe for an explanation, but Wolfe is silent, wearing a proud smirk.

"Is that a Latovian stone in her ring?" Lathe asks.

Wolfe nods, "Yeah. She's able to channel her magic through it when she's outside of Latovia, and on the new moon, she's already stronger. Ashley's power is stronger than Emily's, but she is still learning to control it, and her emotions and stubbornness keep interfering with our training. At least she's not as fucked up as Emily."

Lathe glares at him.

From his seat at the back of the room, Jerrick says, "That isn't Emily. It's like her mind created a separate entity to protect her while she sleeps. It's ruthless, and given a chance; this Emily will destroy Ashley's mind too."

Lathe defends, "Ashley is smart. She wouldn't go in there without a plan."

"I hope so," Jerrick comments, leaving Lathe feeling unsure.

Lathe looks back to the screen when he hears Ashley scream. He watches as she dodges another blow from Emily.

Ashley shouts, "What's the goal here, Emily? You can't beat me with your mind, and you're not gonna win with your physical power. Also, we're like friends."

"I don't want friends!" Emily's voice is flat and droning—zombie-like.

It's the first time they've heard her voice in this state.

"But you will when you wake up," Ashley says, jumping back.

Emily tilts her head and leaps forward. "I don't care," she says before landing on the other side of Ashley.

Ashley spins to face her. "Emily cares. You think this is protecting you, but it's hurting you."

"Shut up!" Emily screams, shooting flames from her palm as the air in the room warms.

Lathe watches the temperature gauge rise above ninety. Ashley wipes the sweat from her eyes and removes her jacket. The fitted pink tank top beneath clings to her sticky skin as she lays the jacket on the wet floor and sits on it.

Wolfe steps toward the monitor. "What is she doing?"

Emily attacks, hitting the purple bubble that surrounds Ashley, while Ashley picks at her nails. "You know, Em, I kinda wish you were this feisty when we worked together. Could you imagine? Eric would say something inappropriate and you'd go all Hulk Smash on him. But this? You attacking me. It's not your best look. And that's the tea."

Emily screams outside the bubble as her flames grow.

Ashley shakes her head. "Whether or not you want to hear it, it's the truth. That's what friends do."

Emily continues to attack without success while Ashley braids her hair, sitting safely inside her purple bubble.

When finished braiding, Ashley asks, "Does that look even to you? It's hard to tell without a mirror." She unwinds the braid and pulls her hair up into a bun on top of her head. As the temperature rises over one-hundred degrees, Lathe blasts the air conditioning, but it struggles to keep up.

"The heat is a nice change from Latovia," Ashley comments. "It's so cold down there, and you know I'm a summer girl."

For the next forty-five minutes, she tries talking to a belligerent Emily who continues to attack. As the temperature continues to climb, Ashley stands and ties her jacket around her waist before walking to the door. They can't open it while Emily is still attacking, so Ashley turns around and strikes out with her magic. The purple bolt of power throws Emily back, stunning her long enough for Ashley to escape the room.

When she enters the control room, Lathe is there waiting for her. "Are you okay?" he asks.

"Yeah." She wipes the sweat from her forehead. "Just hot and frustrated I couldn't get through to her."

He leans in to kiss her as Jerrick announces, "We have a problem."

"What's that?" Wolfe asks.

"Mark Burk is here."

Ashley pulls back from Lathe. "Does he come here often?"

"No, and he never drops by unexpected," Jerrick says while he flips to a multi-screen surveillance feed.

"Has he been trying to call Emily?" Lathe asks.

"No."

Ashley asks, "Does he know about this room?"

"No," Lathe says.

"I think he does now," Jerrick says. "He's on the base-ment stairs."

"Shit."

Wolfe shrugs. "What's the big deal?"

"It's Emily's father."

"Right, but you guys act like you're afraid of him. He's just human."

"Mark is an ally," Jerrick says, "He's someone we want to keep as an ally. And Emily will kill us all if we get on his bad side."

"How much you wanna bet Patrick paid him a visit?" Lathe says.

"He's here." Jerrick moves to the door just as Mark knocks. Jerrick grits his teeth, arranges a pleasant smile, and opens it for him.

MARK BURSTS IN. "Patrick came to see me today."

"Fucking Patrick," Lathe says under his breath.

Mark walks to the surveillance screen. "He wanted to know how Emily was doing. He seemed surprised that I had no idea what he was talking about."

"It's Olvasho business," Wolfe says with a dismissive shrug.

Mark laughs. "Which means it's my business since my daughter leads the Olvasho, and since I help with nearly all of this kind of surveillance."

"We are keeping her safe," Jerrick assures.

Mark takes note of the television screen, seeing Emily. "That's your version of safe?"

"It's all self-inflicted," Lathe says. "If we let her out, she could kill all of us."

"Let me in there," Mark demands.

Jerrick shakes his head. "We can't do that. It's too much of a risk. If something happens to you, she'd never forgive herself, or us."

Mark takes a menacing step toward Jerrick. "Did she hurt Maggie?"

"No."

"Because Maggie was in her life before this chaos began."

"So was Ashley," Lathe justifies.

"Did she hurt Ashley?"

"She tried," Ashley says.

Mark thinks for a moment, saying, "But she probably can sense your magic. I have no magic. There is no reason for her to attack me."

After a beat of silence, Lathe says, "No."

Ashley adds, "You'd be a sitting duck."

Jerrick shakes his head. "It's not safe."

Wolfe shrugs. "There are worse ways to die."

Losing his patience, Mark shouts, "Let me see my daughter!"

They exchange glances.

"NOW!" he demands.

On the screen, everything floating in the war room falls to the floor and Emily's body stills. Her dilated pupils stare into a camera on the ceiling. One of the cameras she hadn't destroyed.

"She knows I'm here," Mark comments.

"We're going in with you," Lathe says, looking to Jerrick for confirmation.

Jerrick gives a nod of agreement.

Ashley pushes forward. "I should be the one to go in with him. She can't manipulate me."

They open the door, and Mark enters the war room.

Flames suddenly consume Emily's body as she lifts into the air. She attacks, but Ashley throws up a shield and the fireball ricochets. Emily's feet touch down, and she runs forward, her flames receding as the wind dies down. Ashley stands at the ready.

Mark moves forward. "Don't you dare stop her."

Ashley prepares to fight, but Emily runs straight past her, tears falling down her soot-covered face as she cries, "Daddy." She throws herself at Mark, the impact pushing him back a step and knocking the wind out of him. His arms fall around her while her arms stay tight around his neck. "I'm so scared, daddy."

Tears come to his eyes as he reassuringly runs a hand over her head. "You're safe now."

Mark closes his eyes, realizing what's going on. She hadn't called him daddy since she was a young child—since before the bad stuff.

THE SUMMER DAY WAS FLAWLESS, *without a cloud in the sky. It was no wonder Emily wanted to stop at the park. But it wasn't the beautiful day that compelled four-year-old Emily*

to beg her parents to stop at the playground.

"Mommy, I want to play with the princess."

"What princess?"

Emily pointed at a brown-haired girl who was playing in the sand with a boy.

"She's a little older than you," Selma said, "but you can ask her if she wants to play."

"When I'm older, we will be best friends, and then I can say my best friend is a princess. Maybe I can marry her twin brother, and then I can be a princess too."

"So, they're royalty?" her mom asked with a chuckle.

"Yeah, their dad is the king."

"Doesn't that make their mom the queen?"

Emily observed the woman sitting on the bench near the siblings. She was beautiful, but with a careful look, Emily answered, "No, she isn't. The king is a bad man. He has dozens of kids, and—" she gasped, "No!"

"Emily," Selma said, trying to remain calm even as her four-year-old started hyperventilating. Selma wrapped Emily in a hug. "It's okay. You're safe now."

"You're safe now," Mark says.

Emily gasps, pulling out of her dad's arms—her adoptive father, but she hadn't known that before.

She keeps backing up, taking in the room. "Dad, what are you doing here?" She spots Ashley standing in a purple haze. "Ashley?" Her breath catches. "I'm so sorry."

The purple haze disappears as Ashley steps forward. "It's okay."

But Emily knows it's not okay, Ashley just doesn't understand why she's apologizing.

Lathe and Jerrick enter the room, stealing Emily's attention. She straightens her spine and wipes away her tears. "Is it morning?"

Lathe and Jerrick look cautious of her, exchanging a look before turning their attention to Mark.

"How did you do that?" Lathe asks.

Mark looks over Emily, her messy hair, soot-covered skin, and confusion. "Emily, you were in a fugue state. This isn't the first time something like this has happened. I wish you guys had said something sooner."

He steps closer to Emily. "Remember when I said your mom had moments of confusion and spouted all kinds of crazy theories. We started recording the things she said, so we could write them down and try to make sense of them."

Emily can't seem to shake off this lingering feeling of dread. "Yeah, you've been sending me mom's journals."

"It wasn't just your mom. It was mostly you. It started when you were four. We were driving through Columbus, and you insisted we had to stop at this park off the beaten path. Your mother and I had no idea how you knew about it, and you said it came to you in a vision. That is where you first saw Ashley and her brother Jacob."

Ashley pales, turning wide-eyed toward Emily.

Emily's chin trembles. Her eyes shimmer with moisture as the memory sits at the forefront of her mind.

Mark places a reassuring hand on Emily's arm. "You knew impossible things, that even your mother had no way of knowing. It's like you were looking into a crystal ball."

"It wasn't a crystal ball." Emily shakes her head, whispering, "It was Evelyn."

Mark nods. "She built a connection with you, a bridge into her mind, so you saw all kinds of things. Things I don't think she intended for you to see. There was death and torture, and every time you connected, it triggered you to go into a fugue state. You acted completely different. Your voice and mannerisms changed, almost like you weren't there at all. And you remembered nothing afterward. Your mother eventually found a way to transfer the connection to her, but it took years, and eventually, she severed the connection all together because Evelyn became too unpredictable."

Emily takes a therapeutic breath. "Why am I just now finding out about this?"

"I didn't mean to keep it from you, but even after your memories were restored, those memories never returned, and it didn't seem important. I thought the visions served their purpose, and that Evelyn destroyed those traumatizing memories. Did she ever say anything about it?"

"No, but if I'd known, I would have asked. Evelyn is the reason Ashley and I met."

"She guided a lot of our life."

Wolfe enters the room, his long dreads pulled back out of his face. The long black dragon skin jacket and pants looking out of place among the casually dressed group. He interrupts, his voice gruff, "As fun as this is, can we circle back to how we can fix what's happening now?"

Mark looks him over, asking, "Who is this guy?"

"I'm Wolfe, king of Latovia."

Mark steps forward. "I'm Mark, father of Emily. Is it true

that Latovian armies created dragons by feeding them children?"

Wolfe gives a hardy laugh. "Dragons never ate people, but perhaps if they had, they'd have survived."

Mark moves toward him with narrowed eyes. "So, none survived?"

"Dead, every last one. My predecessor made no effort to save them. He believed that screwing his way across the country and watching his children die in vain was the better bet."

"And here I am, princess of Latovia." Ashley curtsies. "But how exactly is this helping Emily?"

Emily wraps her arms around herself and glances around for Patrick before remembering he's not there. He'd left her. Her eyes close while she gathers herself. "Lathe, you need to take over as acting leader of the Olvasho. All I'm doing is distracting you from the main objective, which is to find a way to free the Latovian people safely. Fixing me will take time, and Latovia doesn't have time."

Lathe stares at her for a moment before nodding. "Only until you return."

"Okay, but I can't stay here. It's not safe, and it's eating up all of your time."

Jerrick steps forward. "Nowhere else is better equipped."

Wolfe adds, "And the Latovian Portal is here."

Emily looks to Lathe, who purses his lips, his brows pinched. "They're right. This is the best place for you."

"I don't want to be a distraction."

"Then figure this out," Wolfe says, turning to walk out of the room. "I have more important things to do."

Ashley rolls her eyes as she watches him leave. "Which is

Latovian speak for get well soon. Latovians aren't known for their manners."

"Manners are just a pathetic form of flattery," Wolfe shouts from the other room.

Ashley rolls her eyes, shouting, "You're so right, your royal highness." She shakes her head and more quietly says, "Royal pain in my ass. You should've seen the way he reacted when I called him a dick. And he accuses me of being emotional. Ha. He's so determined to save Latovia, but acts like a jerk to the people who can help. I never thought I'd be the polite one." She shrugs. "I actually have to go with him, though." She surprises Emily with a hug before she and Lathe leave the room.

Mark moves with them, saying, "I'll be back. I need to talk to Wolfe."

Once it's only Emily and Jerrick, he says, "I think this is a mistake. You should be the priority right now."

She looks up at him towering over her, focusing on his kind blue eyes rather than his goliath physique. "I can't be. Besides, we don't know what will help."

"I think I know what may help you."

"What?"

"Sit down."

Trust is earned, and Jerrick had won her trust a hundred times over, so without asking why, she lowers herself to the cement floor, sitting cross-legged.

Jerrick sits in front of her. "Hold out your hands and close your eyes."

She places her hand on her knees, palms up, and closes her eyes.

"Slow your breathing." He places his hands in hers.

She blows out a breath, feeling a tingle through her body before her pulse slows and everything around her fades. "Jerrick?" she says, wondering if he's still there. When she doesn't get a return answer, she tries to open her eyes, but her lids are too heavy, her body moving so slowly, her pulse an unhurried rhythm.

MARK RUSHES past Lathe and Ashley and catches up to Wolfe on the basement steps, demanding, "I want you to take me to Latovia."

Wolfe turns to him. "Why?"

"You know why. I think you're hiding something."

"Latovia is a network of caves. It would take months to inspect them all, and I could still hide things from you, so seeing Latovia will not change your suspicion. Either you trust me or you don't, but I don't care either way because I don't need your trust."

Ashley says, "You'll have to excuse him, he has, in fact, lived under a rock his whole life."

Lathe senses power in the war room and hesitates. "Uh."

Wolfe turns to continue his ascent. "Ashley, feel free to show him around Latovia."

Lathe groans, moving down the stairs into the control room. The door to the war room is still wide open and Lathes glimpses Jerrick and Emily before the door slams shut. "Shit."

He rushes over and pulls up the camera feed to find Emily and Jerrick sitting on the floor facing one another. A breeze blows Emily's hair off her shoulders just before she begins floating, her legs still crossed under her and her hands resting on her knees. Jerrick stands and takes a few steps back.

"What's going on?" Ashley says, looking over his shoulder.

"Did you lock her back in?" Mark asks, coming into the room.

"Jerrick did it." Lathe scrolls through the cameras to get the best angle. "He's in there with her."

"Open the door."

Staring at the screen, Lathe says, "I can't. Jerrick is shaking his head. He doesn't want us in there."

"How did he close it?" Ashley asks.

"There is a pocket of water inside the door which allows Patrick and Jerrick to open and close it. It's a safety feature."

"Why would he lock us out without telling us?" Marks asks.

"I don't know."

SUBDUE AND CONFESS

10

EMILY OPENS HER EYES SLOWLY, the cool breeze refreshing against her skin. She rolls to her side, only to feel something rough like sandpaper against her arm. Looking at the slanted surface, she realizes she's lying on a roof. She sits up just as the sun peeks over the horizon. It reflects on the lake behind the mansion.

"How did I get here?" she asks herself, not expecting an answer.

"You wanted to feel free," Evelyn says from behind her, moving down the roof in her sundress and snow boots.

Emily can't break her focus from those boots. The same boots Evelyn wore when she thought she hit her with her car a year ago.

She takes a seat next to Emily, saying, "I thought you'd like the boots."

Emily looks up in time to witness Evelyn's smile melt away. "I never meant to cause you so much pain."

"It seems we both made mistakes," Selma says, sitting down on the other side of Emily.

"Mom," Emily breathes, moving to give her a hug. When she pulls back, she asks, "What are you both doing here?"

"We're not really here," says Selma.

"We're a figment of your imagination," Evelyn adds, "But we live on inside of you so long as you carry us with you."

Selma runs her fingers through Emily's hair. "But we can be a burden to hold. We remind you of what you've lost, but this is not the end. You'll see us again."

"So, why am I seeing you now?"

Evelyn answers, "We're here because your mind is trying to fix itself."

"We're here to help you," Selma says. "Think of it as talk therapy. We'll help you modify your reactions to psychological distress."

"And how are you going to help me, if you are just extensions of my imagination?"

Selma lifts her hand, palm up, and a flame dances across its surface. "Because you've got magic."

Evelyn leans in, whispering, "Loads of it."

Selma smiles. "And you have felt our spirits in your mind."

"You're tapping into them now so we can guide you," Evelyn adds.

"Sometimes it will be excruciating, and you'll try to kick us out of your head. Don't. It may feel easier to live with the pain than to face it, but to improve, you must keep going," Selma urges. "For yourself. For your fellow Olvasho. For Latovia."

Selma leans closer, whispering, "For Patrick."

"He left me." Emily avoids her gaze as she fights her tears.

Selma moves her hair out of her face. "You triggered his past trauma."

"He had to leave," Evelyn says. "It's for the best."

Evelyn adds, "You need to learn how to live without him. Rely on yourself before anyone."

Emily stands, turning away. "Both of you relied on others."

Evelyn stays in her spot, twisting toward Emily. "We aren't saying that you'll always be alone. We all need others. But you have to know how to be alone."

Selma comes up behind her, whispering over her shoulder. "Patrick can't restore you. Only you can do that."

Emily turns toward them. "So, what do we do first?"

Evelyn pats the spot next to her. "Let's go back to the beginning."

Emily takes a seat next to Evelyn, looking back out at the water, watching how the breeze creates gentle waves that lap at the shore. Selma sits next to her, prompting, "You were four years old. We were driving when Evelyn showed you a vision of Ashley. She guided you to the playground where you saw Ashley and Jacob and knew they were Latovian royalty. You knew about the king, and then what happened?"

Emily frowns, a groove forming between her eyebrows. "I saw his children die. I watched their skin petrify. Some died slowly, and some shoved into the sun by their father, an instant death. Jacob and Ashley petrified, dying slowly."

Evelyn lays a hand reassuringly on her back. "And what did you do?"

Emily turns to her. "You showed me I could save one of them. They each had the potential for magic, but not enough to keep them alive, so I shifted Jacob's magic to Ashley."

"Yes. But why Ashley? Why not Jacob?" Selma asks.

"Evelyn showed me the future. Latovians forced Jacob and Wolfe to fight to the death. I watched Jacob behead Wolfe, but Latovia will crumble without him as their king."

EMILY IS LEVITATING, legs crossed, hands on her knees. The soft breeze flows around the room. And Jerrick circles below, keeping Emily's heartbeat steady, keeping her in a subdued state. He'd planned on guided imagery, taking the form of Evelyn, hoping it would help Emily feel more comfortable, but he hadn't expected Selma. Emily is doing that on her own.

Jerrick prompts, "Why Ashley? Why not Jacob?"

"Evelyn showed me the future. Latovians forced Jacob and Wolfe to fight to the death. I watched Jacob behead Wolfe, but Latovia will crumble without him as their king."

Knowing how much guilt Ashley carries about her twin's death, Jerrick looks up to the camera, hoping Ashley can find some closure.

"I WATCHED JACOB BEHEAD WOLFE, but Latovia will crumble without him as their king."

The control room is absolutely silent. Mark, Lathe, and Ashley stand mesmerized, afraid to breathe too loud for fear they will miss a word from the monitor in front of them. Ashley's trembling hands cover her mouth as tears cloud her eyes.

Jerrick looks up at the camera with a look of sympathy before turning back toward Emily and asking, "Did she show you the future with Ashley?"

Emily hesitates, the groove between her eyes deepening before she nods, saying, "The Latovian people accepted her as their queen."

"Queen?" Ashley breathes.

In the war room, Jerrick asks Emily, "What about Wolfe?"

"They married, and together they stood as king and queen of Latovia."

Ashley pales. "What?"

After a long pause, Jerrick asks, "You saw them get married?"

"Latovians don't have weddings. They get three tattoo bands on their left wrists as a symbol of an everlasting commitment."

Ashley looks down at her new tattoos. "What the fuck?"

Lathe grabs her hand, pulling it toward him. "I thought this was to warn you of petrifying."

"It is," Wolfe's gruff voice comes from the hall.

They spin, finding him leaning against the doorframe. Ashley rushes over to him, yanking up his left sleeve, and there mixed with all his older tattoos are three bands around his left wrist.

She steps back, gaping at him. "You lied to me."

Wolfe steps forward. "Relax, we're only married in

Latovia, and the magic won't take effect unless we consummate our bond. It's not a big deal."

A violent gust of wind shoves Wolfe into the wall, and Lathe steps between Ashley and Wolfe. "If it's not a big deal, then why hide it?"

Ashley steps forward. "And what else are you hiding?"

With a twisted scowl, Wolfe pushes against the air current, growling, "It's not like you didn't know this is how it would go. Your mom warned you. It was always the way it was going to happen."

Ashley grabs Lathe's shoulder and forces him to look at her. "You knew?"

He winces. "My mother told me you would be the queen of Latovia. It's one reason I didn't want to get involved with you, but what we have . . . I thought we could change the future."

"Does Deja know?"

"Deja knows everything, but she—"

"Hey!" Mark yells, "Listen!" He turns up the volume on the monitor.

". . . Latovian magic will lead them to feed their young to the dragons. Dragons and their sorcerers will take over everything you see. Fire will rain down from the sky as their unquenchable desire for power propels them to consume every living being."

"Good Lord!" Mark curses, falling back into a chair. "She saw all of this when she was four years old." He rubs his head. "I see why she suppressed it. Dammit Evelyn."

"Watch it," Lathe warns. "My mother had incredible gifts, but her mind was a mess. She was a victim like the rest of us."

On the monitor, Jerrick asks, "Your Olvasho abilities have always been strong, even as a child, you had more abilities than most adults. I mean, you shifted the magic in the twins. Why didn't you use your gifts more frequently?"

"I only knew how to use my gift when you were with me?"

"She thinks she's talking to Evelyn," Ashley says.

Emily rubs at her face, her movements slow. "I'm exhausted now. I need to rest."

"Yes, I think that's a good idea. We'll talk again soon. Whenever you need us."

Ashley and Lathe turn back to confront Wolfe, but he's gone.

WOLFE LEANS AGAINST A TREE, staying out of view of the mansion as he looks out at the lake, seeing only the brightest stars reflecting off the calm water. "I can feel you hovering," he says, lifting his chin and inhaling the fresh air. "I see you're anticipating my moves now."

"You've become predictable, old man," Deja says as she swings down from a branch above.

"And you're becoming sloppy. Where did you get a red shirt?"

"Ashley gave it to me."

Wolfe grumbles under his breath.

"I told you, you should've talked to her," Deja says.

"How much did you hear?"

"I was in the vent, so most of it." She bends down to pick a dandelion.

"She's mad at you too."

"She'll forgive me," she says, standing. "I'm adorable, and I'm not the one who secretly married her." She pushes back her jet-black hair and blows dandelion seeds into the breeze. "I'm just following orders from my king, even if he is a dumbass."

He could kill her for the way she talks to him, but she only does it when no one is around, and he appreciates how real she is with him. "You know you won't be adorable forever."

"No, but I have other skills, and who knows, maybe I'll be beautiful like Ashley, and all the stupid boys in Latovia will start killing each other over me."

"She's your queen now."

"She's not my queen. She loves Lathe, which means you'll never complete your bond."

"Since you're so adorable, I need you to explain to Ashley and Lathe why I did it."

She nods, but then purses her lips. "I don't like lying to Lathe."

"It won't be for much longer."

"What if he stops trusting me?"

"He won't stop loving you. I would do it, but you know I have somewhere to be." He turns away.

"Wolfe," she says tentatively, "they keep having all these predictions about dragons."

Wolfe turns back and kneels to eye-level with her. "Deja, I'll do my best to protect you, but I promise, dragons are the least of our concern."

He rises, but Deja calls, "Wolfe." When he hesitates, she says, "Don't die."

"You remember what to do if I don't come back?"

Her shoulders slump, and chin falls as she nods.

"Good." With that, he walks off into the moonless night, and Deja turns back toward the mansion.

DEJA ENTERS through the back door, not bothering to be sneaky since she needs to talk to Ashley and Lathe, but she wasn't expecting to be rushed by them as soon as she entered the house.

"Deja, did you know Wolfe and I are married?"

Deja keeps walking, steering them away from the back doors of the mansion. "You aren't married. It just looks like you are. He did it to save lives, not because he loves you or anything."

Ashley walks with her. "What?"

Deja stops. "You hate Latovian culture, which is why he didn't tell you. He didn't want you to dislike Latovia more than you already do."

"I don't hate Latovia."

Deja plants a hand on her hip and tilts her head to the side. "You call us barbaric at least twenty times a day. You think it's barbaric to have children living in stone bunks. You think it's barbaric to challenge the king to fight to the death. You dishonor the king like ten times a day, and he lets you, even though people are watching. He had to make them think there was a reason you could talk to him the way you do. You don't understand the Latovian culture and I don't think you want to, but since you asked, I'll tell you. You're beautiful and powerful. If Wolfe hadn't married you, Latovians would kill each other, trying to win your attention. I mean that literally, which you probably think is barbaric, which is why Wolfe didn't tell you."

Ashley rolls her eyes with a sigh. "I get your point, but it is barbaric."

Deja presses her lips together and shakes her head. "Wolfe has been working to change things since before I was born and he has had to do a lot of barbaric things because if he tries to change things too drastically, people won't follow him. So he's doing it slowly, trying to keep the most people alive."

"Deja," Lathe says in his intimidatingly calm voice. "Why isn't Wolfe here to tell us this?"

"He wanted to avoid a fight."

"Lie," Lathe says.

"He had some king stuff to do.

"Lie!"

Ashley chimes in, "Technically, everything he does is king stuff."

Deja points to Ashley. "See, she gets it."

"WHERE IS HE?" A burst of wind rattles everything on the walls.

Deja's eyes go round, her pale face going ghostly. Ashley gives him a sideways glance, placing a hand on his arm, but he brushes her off and steps toward Deja. "The next time you lie to me, I'm kicking you out. I won't let you visit anymore."

Deja's lips narrow, her little chin quivering as her eyes shimmer.

"Lathe," Ashley breathes, trying to pull him back, but Lathe doesn't break his angry stare.

Deja swallows, her chin rising to him. "I'm leaving anyway. And don't worry, I won't be back." She rushes off.

Lathe stares at the floor while his teeth grind and his head shakes. "Fuck," he growls, going after her, but he knows she's already long gone when he gets to the basement and there is no sign of her. She has a knack for hiding. Knowing he'll never find her, he goes back to Ashley in the kitchen.

TRUST

11

Wolfe's mother taught him how to sew when he was a young child and ever since, he's made his own clothing. His mother always imparted practical skills while his father encouraged Wolfe to think bigger and better.

Few Latovian children were educated. Customarily kids learned a trade and worked in that business until they died, but Wolfe's dad was a dreamer. He filled their family's dwelling with books, and Wolfe learned to read and write at a young age. He was an intelligent and thoughtful child.

His father warned people about Latovia's dying magic. And once Latovians began questioning king Mazilon about Latovia's future, the king took it as a challenge, and the only time you challenged the king was with a fight to the death. Wolfe's father was not a fighter and refused to defend himself.

He died quickly.

Feeling such little satisfaction with the win, the king took it out on Wolfe's mother by forcing her out into the sun.

Seven-year-old Wolfe was forced to go with her and witness her death.

Afterward, he met Evelyn, the first Olvasho he'd ever met. His father had told him about the Olvasho and that most of them were not the monsters the king preached. Evelyn was kind to him. She took him in and comforted the grieving child until he was ready to go back to Latovia.

When Wolfe went back, he moved into the orphan's bunks. His parents ingrained many things that have helped Wolfe, but he had to teach himself how to fight. He quickly understood that in order to survive, he must become ruthless and cunning. He became a true professional at watching his back, and right now, he feels Ashley watching him. She has been stalking him since he returned to Latovia early this morning.

He knows why she's so angry. Lying about marrying her wasn't the best way to earn trust, but her watching his every move is pissing him off, especially as he drapes the black dragon skin pelts over his arm. He counts out twenty-five and then heads toward the market.

Every Sunday, the main Cavern became a trade market, filled mostly with handmade goods and foods. Ashley follows in his shadow, but she's not a good spy. No way would she survive Latovia without him.

As he delivers the uncut dragon skin, Ashley blends into the crowd, but Wolfe finds her a little while later. He stands back and observes her as she questions people at the Sunday market.

The two men she's talking to are eyeing her body when Wolfe approaches. "Ashley," he says—a warning in his voice.

The men look down or away from Ashley, fearing Wolfe will get the impression they are challenging him.

"Thanks for your time," Ashley says to the men who will no longer look at her.

As she spins toward Wolfe, he warns, "Stop searching."

"Or what?" With a cocked brow, she tilts her head to the side, challenging, "You'll marry me." She walks away from him, but he follows her out of the crowd.

After turning a corner, Ashley spins on him. "Are you following me around now?"

"Word got back to me that you are still asking about dragons."

Her eyes narrow. "Kind of a gossipy group, aren't they?"

Wolfe takes a step closer. "You are the only one stirring the gossip."

"Oh, please." She rolls her eyes.

He takes another step closer. "I would've been within my rights to murder those men for looking at you the way they did."

"Fuck you, and your misogynistic ways."

"I don't discriminate. If a woman looked at you the way those men were, I have the same right."

Ashley puts a hand to her hip. "Actually, you don't because we aren't actually married, Wolfe."

He steps closer. "Is that a proposal to make it official?"

"It's a proposal to fuck off."

He shoves her against the cave wall, forearm at her throat, growling, "This isn't a fucking joke!"

Wolfe watches as Ashley's nostrils flare and her inky eyes take on a purple glint. He feels the whisper of her magic tingling across his skin. A clear warning, and an exciting preview of what she's capable of. He's thrilled with the control she has over it, owning every inch of her magic. She's been holding back. The kind of deception that speaks of her Latovian blood.

Wolfe barely holds in his smile.

Ashley's voice is carefully measured and threatening. "Let go of me."

Wolfe leans in, whispering, "Make me."

"Now who's acting like a child?"

His voice turns grave. "You're the child. Are you doing this to get back at me for marrying you? Is that why you're spreading the idea of dragons? Did you know if enough of them believe dragons still exist, it will give the idea power? Now act like the fucking queen you're supposed to be and stop putting ideas into people's heads."

She glares up at him, her irises darker than any he's ever seen, like black holes that would suck him in if he gets too close. He is already too close, but the discomfort doesn't sway him from his position.

With her chin raised, her breath tickles against his jaw. "Where did you get the dragon pelts, Wolfe? There were dozens of them."

His head falls back. "You're obsessed." He runs a hand down his face. "Kings have been known to hoard dragon skin. There are hundreds in there. I try to bring them out a few at a time, but the truth is, we don't have much longer in Latovia, so I may as well bring them out. We won't always be stuck in these dank, dark caves."

"You're so sure we'll get out."

He shrugs. "We'll get out or we'll die. Either way, there won't be a need for dragon skin."

"So, all of those dragon skins are old?"

He pulls back. "Jesus fuck, Ashley! Do you want it written in blood?"

"I want proof that they're all dead. Show me their bones or something."

He grinds his jaw and flexes his hands, unsure how Lathe tolerates her constant attitude. He takes a breath and pinches the bridge of his nose. "They were cremated. The dragons did it to each other, and when they became too sick to incinerate each other, we torched them out of respect."

"That's a little too convenient."

He lets his arms fall to his sides in exhaustive surrender. "Why don't you believe me?"

Her eyebrows pinch and she lets out a silent breath. He watches her shoulders deflate. It's fractional, but he doesn't miss the shift in her rigid posture. She bites her lip and looks at the stone floor beneath their feet. "I just feel like you're lying."

He shakes his head. "Have I been that terrible to you?"

"No."

"So why don't you believe me?"

She glances up at him with those dark as sin, doe eyes, and whispers, "I can't explain it."

He reaches for her, appealing to her softer side by curling his calloused palms around her soft, delicate hands. "Try."

"I can't," she snaps, pulling from his grip and rushing off.

PROCEED WITH CAUTION

12

LATHE RUNS a hand over his freshly shaved scalp before pulling his hood up and entering the control room. He takes a seat next to Jerrick, asking, "Did Mark step out?"

"He had to make some calls. He'll be back."

Lathe observes the monitor, watching Emily float in the middle of the room in a modified lotus position with fire burning a circle around her. "At least she looks calm."

Jerrick nods. "She did it on her own this time. Her mom is probably helping to guide her through her memories, but she didn't seem to need Evelyn. I'm monitoring her in case something goes wrong."

After a beat of silence, Lathe says, "Thanks for being here, even if it is to punish yourself for what happened to your family. The Olvasho are lucky to have you."

"Emily is my family now, and I won't let her die."

"You know, everything Patrick said was true. We're all murderers. I never thanked you for holding me back the day my mother was killed."

Jerrick glances over at him. "I wasn't doing it for you."

"I know, but I'm still glad you stopped me from killing anyone else."

Jerrick nods and they both stare at Emily, mumbling to herself, too quiet to make out the words.

While looking at the monitor, Lathe says, "You know, Keith is missing, and two of his known associates are suddenly in prison without trial. They say you had something to do with his disappearance." He glances at Jerrick. "What happened there?"

Jerrick continues watching Emily. "Keith went after Morgan. I believe in mercy, so I gave his associates some time in prison so they could reflect on how they lost their way."

"Does Emily know?"

Jerrick shifts his gaze to Lathe. "No."

"You can't just kill whoever you want."

He turns back to the screen. "I assure you, I can. But I won't. Keith's death was justified."

Lathe smirks. "How many people have you justified?"

"Only the ones who would keep killing."

"I don't want you turning into a serial killer, even if you're only murdering other serial killers."

"Like Dexter."

Lathe narrows his eyes. "Who?"

"Never mind."

Lathe sighs. "None of us are innocent, but I don't want any of us turning into my father."

Jerrick turns his full glare at Lathe. "I don't have a desire for power or a murderous impulse. I do not kill because I'm full of rage or because I enjoy it. I don't get a high from it. I'm a sniper in a world of foot soldiers. You may not see the whole picture, but I do, and I take out the threat with precision before they attack again."

Lathe stares ahead, watching his half-sister float in a room mumbling to what he can only assume is her dead mother, who is leading her back through suppressed memories. "Well, what do you know, Patrick was right. We're all majorly fucked up."

Jerrick's gaze returns to the monitor. "She's in love with him."

"I know." Lathe nods. "Do you think he's coming back?"

With a headshake, Jerrick says, "Only time will tell."

The air around Emily begins circulating, feeding the flames that surround her.

Lathe stands. "That's not good."

Jerrick is already on his way to the war room door.

"You can't go in there with her like that."

Jerrick types in the code to unlock the door. "She's making progress. If she loses control, it's a huge step backward and who knows what that would mean. Just keep the fire off me so I can slow her heart rate. Once I get her calmed down, you can leave."

Lathe nods, following him into the burning room.

EMILY TILTS HER CHIN UP, her eyes drawn to the intricate gold detail covering the ceiling—the handcrafted design from a bygone era.

There is something about this lobby, something about this hotel that feels familiar. She can't recall being here before, yet she knows there is supposed to be a modern chandelier hanging in place of the gaudy gold ceiling, and the front desk is on the wrong side of the lobby.

She gasps, remembering how she knows this place. Last time she was here, she had just stolen two tigers. "Mom, why did you bring me here? I don't want to be here."

"This is where you first met Patrick. It's why you came here when Adelaide possessed your body."

Emily backs up, shaking her head. "I don't want to be here."

Her mom stands in front of her, gripping her shoulders to focus her attention. "Emily, if you don't do this, things will not improve."

Emily shakes her head as fat tears roll down her cheeks. "That's okay. It's not that bad."

She pulls out of Selma's grip and runs across the lobby and out the revolving glass door. The blistering cold Chicago wind stings her skin as she runs down the sidewalk.

A massive man steps into her path out of nowhere and she runs right into him, knocking her down. Almost immediately, a hand reaches down to help her to her feet. Emily stares at the hand, feeling dazed.

"Emily, dear, you can't run from yourself forever."

Emily looks up to find Evelyn standing above her. She takes her outstretched hand, feeling a soothing warmth that protects her from the blistering cold.

"Come, let's go back to the hotel."

"But I don't want to remember this," Emily sobs.

"But you already do remember it. It haunts your subconscious. The longer you keep it hidden, the more time it has to pollute the rest of you. It's better to cut out the infection than for it to fester and grow."

She takes a shaky breath. "I'm . . . scared."

"It's okay to be afraid. I'll be with you the whole time."

"I don't want my mom to know—only you. You told me not to tell anyone, remember? It's our secret."

With a hesitant nod, Evelyn wraps her arm around Emily's shoulder and leads her back to the hotel. This time when they enter, Selma is absent.

The tarnished gold ceilings, brown water stained surfaces, and peeling wallpaper are all evidence of long-standing neglect. A woman wearing a red mini dress, fishnet stockings, and hooker heels strokes her hand down a man's chest, clutching at the lapel of his business suit. The man hands cash to the desk clerk in exchange for a room key.

When the couple turns and walks by Emily, the cigarette smoke is overpowering. It burns Emily's eyes, tickles her nose, and makes her head ache.

She chokes and hides her face in her arm, saying, "I see why they renovated."

Evelyn's hand lands on her shoulder. "Emily, focus on why we're here?"

She closes her eyes and says, "I was six when we came here because my mom was meeting someone. My dad waited in the car with Samantha while I went inside with my mom because I had to use the bathroom."

Emily opens her eyes and watches her younger self walking hand in hand with her mother across the lobby. She continues narrating. "She walked me back out to my dad before going back in to meet her friend, but while I was walking through the lobby, I crossed paths with a blond boy."

The boy appears, walking into the lobby beside his father as Emily and her mother were on their way out.

"Our eyes met, triggering all these visions. They were things you had already seen. I saw Patrick kill his mother. I saw what Sky did to him and what he became. My mom had to pick me up and carry me out to the car. And as she carried me out, I just kept staring at young Patrick, his grey-blue eyes looking scared of me. I wanted to tell him—to warn him."

"Why didn't you?" Evelyn prompts.

"I blacked out, and when I woke, you showed me the future where Patrick's family lived, and the world burned."

"It's the only vision you wanted me to keep from my parents. You never meant for me to see it, and you tried to take it away, but your mind fell into disarray and for days, I held Patrick's future and his fate in my head. Eventually, you took the memories, but I carried the guilt. The guilt of letting innocent people die and allowing Patrick to suffer for years.

"To escape, I went to the other place. The place I went to protect myself, where I didn't have to deal with anything bad."

Emily shakes her head. "I can't believe I let him suffer. I caused all of this. We could've prevented it, Evelyn." Emily stands. "How could you let innocent people suffer? How could we do this to Patrick?" Her brows pinch together and her eyes shift, searching for forgiveness or understanding to excuse her behavior. Gripping the sides of her head, she bends double as if the emotional toll hurts her physically.

"How could I?" Those fat tears roll down her cheeks again. Evelyn moves forward to comfort her, but Emily turns away from her.

The hotel disappears. Everything disappears into total blackness.

She feels Evelyn's hand on her shoulder and knows she's

still there, but her grief is all-consuming. She could've stopped it. They would have found a way to keep the world from burning, but instead, Patrick suffered. She tortured him even after he escaped Sky. Now he won't even talk to her, and it hurts. God, does it hurt.

Doesn't he know what he means to her? She looks around in the darkness until she finds him. Adult Patrick is the only thing amid total blackness. He's sitting on a stool, but she can't see anything else like where he is or if he's with anyone.

He's looking down at something, but suddenly turns his head toward her. His eyes widen and he stands so clumsily that his stool falls backward.

Evelyn sucks in a breath, her hand falling from Emily's shoulder.

Emily doesn't have time to acknowledge the woman's retreat. She is too focused on getting to Patrick, who is shaking his head as he backs away. "Emily . . . how?"

She takes a few steps forward.

His eyes flare, his face pales. "Emily?"

"It's okay. I won't hurt you." She reaches out to him only a few feet away.

He steps out of reach, shaking his head. "I don't believe you."

As his image disappears, she shouts, "No!" But he's already gone.

She falls to her knees and sobs.

MORGAN LOOKS at Patrick when he knocks the kitchen stool over. He slides along the counter, backing up like he's seen a ghost.

Chills run down her spine as she stands from the couch. "Patrick?"

He doesn't seem to hear her, instead he's staring straight ahead like he sees something that isn't there. "Emily . . . how?"

Morgan searches the room more fervently, determined to see what he's seeing.

He steps back, shaking his head. "I don't believe you."

Morgan still doesn't see what he's seeing, so she steps in front of him, putting her hands on his shoulders to steal his focus. "Patrick?"

He blinks as if coming back to reality. His shoulders slouch in relief. "Oh, thank God, Morgan." He wraps his arms around her.

EMILY'S MIND slips from Jerrick's connection, and any control he had is completely severed. He eyes her cautiously, finding her standing a few feet away from him in the war room. She tilts her head to the side and Jerrick takes a step away.

"You aren't Evelyn," Emily says, her pupils dilated. "My mommy and daddy don't let me talk to strangers, but you tricked me. You made me think you were Evelyn."

Jerrick flicks his eyes toward the camera, wondering if Mark is back yet. Jerrick keeps taking small steps toward the door, but he won't make it.

Wind whirls around Emily, and Jerrick asks, "What did you do with the other Emily?"

"She was sad, so I'm protecting her."

"I'm her friend. I was helping her."

She shakes her head. "You made her cry. You're all bad for her."

She holds out her hand, waving her fingers as flames dance between them. Jerrick points behind her, indicating someone's presence, and when she turns to look, he sprints toward the door. Arms pumping and legs flying, the door opens as he approaches. He slides through before using his gifts to slam the door behind him. The door vibrates with the impact of Emily's powers.

Jerrick slides across the control room, landing on his hands and knees.

Lathe runs to Jerrick's aid. "What the hell just happened?"

Jerrick falls forward on his arms, and that's when Lathe notices he didn't get out unscathed. The back of his shirt is still smoldering, and the skin beneath is bloody and charred.

Jerrick grits his teeth and buries his head in his hands, groaning, "How bad is it?"

Lathe hesitates, inspecting the gash that extends from Jerrick's left shoulder down to his right lower back. He places his hands on the nauseating wound. "Her flames must have hit you. It's partly cauterized. It's gonna leave a scar."

Jerrick grunts, curling his hands into fists as Lathe begins healing the wound.

Mark enters from the hall and pauses when he sees Jerrick on the floor, his forehead resting on his fisted hands while sweat drips from his face and his teeth grind. Lathe barely shoots Mark a glance before returning all of his attention to Jerrick's open wound. Blood covers his hands as he works on healing him.

"I'm gonna have to rip open the parts that are cauterized," Lathe warns. "Stay still."

"Fuck you. I am still." But he isn't. His body is already shaking with pain.

Mark unfreezes from his stance, saying, "I'll get the morphine." He grabs the emergency kit they'd told him about from the filing cabinet and draws up the morphine. "This stuff is bitter," he warns.

"Just give it to me," Jerrick growls, grabbing the syringe out of Mark's hand and shooting it in his mouth.

Mark moves to the monitors to check on Emily while Lathe opens the burns. Jerrick cries out, and Mark searches through the drawers until he finds a notebook. He takes it to Jerrick, saying, "Bite down on this."

Jerrick grabs it, biting down as he groans through the pain.

After several minutes, Jerrick finally quiets, and Mark asks, "What did you guys do to her?"

Lathe glares at Emily's father. "You mean, what did she do to him?"

Mark looks back at the monitor where Emily is sitting inside a tornado of fire. "I thought she was doing better. What happened?"

"Maybe you shouldn't have left." Lathe suggests, perspiration dotting his forehead as he continues to work on Jerrick.

When Lathe has done all he can do, he sits back on the floor, leaning against the wall.

Jerrick rolls onto his back and takes a breath. "We need to call Patrick. I knew their connection was strong, but if she can get to him like that then . . ."

Lathe stands and paces the room, watching the screen. Emily has calmed down and is curled in a ball on the floor, crying.

Mark types the code in and opens the reinforced concrete door. The inside is completely scorched, and a chunk of the concrete has crumbled away. Mark glances back at Jerrick. "You're lucky to be alive."

FUTURE PLANS

13

Ashley comes through the portal, walking into the underground tunnel. Lathe had worked tirelessly to make the place feel more comfortable. He had arranged a collection of couches between the portal door and the elevator, and he installed large space heaters that warm the area to around seventy degrees. It's balmy compared to Latovia's mid-fifties.

Lathe is fast asleep on his favorite couch. Ashley quietly sets down the bag she's carrying and removes her jacket, draping it over a chair before joining Lathe on the couch. He's on his back, so when she stretches out beside him, his arm automatically wraps around her to pull her closer. She snuggles on top of him, her head against his chest. She listens to the steady beat of his heart.

She sighs, bringing her mouth up to his ear. "I don't want to lose you."

His fingers run up and down her spine. "I'm not going anywhere, sunshine."

"But what if something happens to one of us? It's naive

to think we all will survive when so many people have died over this curse."

His hand stops its movement. "Ashley, look at me."

She lifts her head, exposing the tears clouding her eyes and the fear she can't hide.

His palm gently cradles her face and he lifts his head for a quick kiss, but when he pulls back, Ashley's lips follow. Her tongue meets his and her legs straddle him, her body moving on top of his.

Her touch sets him on fire, and soon he's tugging off her shirt and unbuttoning her jeans. She slows him down by sitting on her heels and slowly sliding her hand under his shirt and pushing it up, exposing his scared masculine chest. Even though he's still self-conscious about the scars running from the top of his head down to his abdomen, Ashley has a way of making him forget his discomfort. She runs her tongue up from his abs to his pecs, teasing him.

He pulls off his shirt and flips them, so Ashley is on the bottom. He tugs at her jeans, and she giggles at his impatience. He pauses once he has her down to her red lacy bra and matching panties. His eyes flick to hers. "You did this for me?"

She stretches out before him with a sultry grin. "Red is your favorite color."

His eyes flare as he watches her. "There are so many things I want to do to you."

She runs a finger down between her breasts down to her panties, where her hand dips below the material.

"Fuck." Lathe loses his own jeans and boxers in one quick movement, and then he's climbing on top of her. His excitement nudges against the lacy material of her panties.

"Aren't you gonna take them off?"

He shakes his head. "Nope." He pushes the flimsy material to the side and slides in with a groan.

"Mmm," Ashley moans while he stills himself deep inside. The connection alone brings so much pleasure, and she's enjoying his struggle to be gentle right now. He loves her. She has no doubt, especially when he's buried inside her and staring at her the way he is right now.

With his crystal blue eyes on her, he says, "Marry me."

She gasps. "What?"

He pulls out slowly, before rocking back in. "Marry me."

She gawks at him, and he repeats the same movement as he uses his hands to tease her nipples through the red lace.

She moves her hips against him, needing him to move faster, needing the friction. "Lathe . . . "

His lips meet hers and her hands wrap around him as she says, "The first thing you need to know as my fiancé is that I'm pissed when I don't get my way. Now, move faster."

He gives her his lopsided grin, and Ashley gets what she asked for, loving the friction and speed. She loves that he makes love like a gentleman but fucks like a beast. She loves his raw masculinity and the softness he hides beneath it. She loves that she gets to see both sides. The immense pleasure is wrapped in so many layers of love. She can't get enough of him.

They trade positions, and she rides him before he flips her around and takes her from behind. But ultimately, they are face to face when they lose themselves to the pleasure.

Afterward, they are lying on the couch together and Lathe says, "That could've been dangerous. What if some kids had come through the portal?"

Ashley shakes her head. "I banned the mansion. With Emily's instability, I didn't think it was safe for kids to be here. Deja is the only kid who would break the rule, but she's still mad at you."

Ashley slips into her pants while Lathe tugs his on. She pulls her shirt over her head, and once it's on, Lathe kneels in front of her holding out a ring.

"Oh my God!" Her hands go to her mouth. "So that wasn't just a totally impulsive proposal?"

Lathe gives her his crooked grin. "It was not how I planned it, but I couldn't wait."

She gets down on her knees in front of him. Placing her hands on his cheeks. "This isn't just because I'm pretend married to Wolfe, is it?"

His smile melts, and he raises an eyebrow as his jaw hardens.

"Oh, God, that face. Okay. Sorry I asked." She leans in to kiss him. When she pulls back, she holds out her left hand, and he slides the ring on her finger.

"This ring belonged to my grandmother."

"The one who fell in love with a Latovian that died from sun poisoning?"

Lathe nods. "We can get a different ring if you want."

"No, this is perfect." Ashley holds out her hand, inspecting the ring. As the clear diamond turns purple, they both become speechless for a moment.

Ashley looks to Lathe. "Did you know it was a Latovian stone?"

He shakes his head. "No, I even had it appraised. They said the cut and clarity of this diamond is very rare and expensive."

"Even the little gems on the side are Latovian." Ashley looks up at Lathe. "The king would have killed your grandfather had he know he took stones out of Latovia."

"Is it cursed? Did I propose with a cursed ring?"

Ashley smiles. "No. I think it's perfect." She stands and pulls him up with her, embracing him for a moment before pushing back. "I have a gift for you too."

"I thought the lingerie was my gift."

She giggles. "That was to help persuade you of this next part."

"Are you using your body as a weapon, sunshine?"

She shrugs with a smirk. "Maybe." She holds up her hand with the ring. "I don't even know if you're allowed to disagree with me at this point."

"I'm your fiancé, not your bitch."

Ashley laughs. "And thank God for that."

"What is it you need to convince me of?"

Ashley fiddles with her ring as she avoids his eyes. "I need you to help me."

Lathe eyes her.

Ashley looks up at him and steps forward. "Wolfe won't approve, so this stays between us." Ashley walks over to the bag she set on the floor. She opens it and pulls out the gallon jar.

Lathe looks horrified. "Please tell me that's not what I think it is."

"A lot of Latovians are dying. Too many. They're afraid and desperate."

"Ashley, how did you get that?"

"Latovia is weird. They have all these barbaric blood magic rituals."

"Ashley, is that a gallon of human blood?" He's shaking his head like he wants her to deny it.

"It's enough for you to enter Latovia."

Lathe turns away, putting his hands to the back of his head.

She sets the jar down and moves toward him. "Wolfe is hiding something."

Lathe spins to her. "How do you know?"

She grimaces, squeezing her eyes shut before admitting, "The magic speaks to me. It whispers to me, but they aren't words. It's more of a feeling."

"A feeling that Wolfe is lying?"

"A feeling that dragons are real. I know it sounds crazy."

He stares at her for a moment, saying, "A lot of things sound crazy, but it doesn't mean they aren't real."

"So, you believe me?"

"Of course, I do." He points over to the blood. "But that?"

"Some Latovians will buy blood to use for forbidden blood magic rituals. When desperate, the underprivileged will bottle their blood and sell it to make a little money. It's super weird and dangerous. If they're caught, they get in a lot of trouble."

"That's not a little bottle."

"After someone dies, they drain their blood and destroy it, but sometimes the blood is stolen and sold. Most people don't like to use blood from the dead. They're very superstitious people. Anyway, this was confiscated by Wolfe from a guy intending to sell it."

"So you want me to cover myself in some dead guys blood and come to Latovia. And then what?"

"Then you see if you can hear the magic I'm talking about. Just pop in the portal. See if you can hear it and then pop out. Wolfe will sense your magic when you enter, but I'll mask it to throw him off. I just don't want to feel like I'm going crazy, but I can't trust him."

Lathe nods. "Fine. When do you want to do this?"

"Well, the blood is actually the backup plan. First, I think we should stage a fight in front of Deja. Once she believes I've broken my connection to you, she'll tell Wolfe, and maybe he'll trust me with whatever he's hiding. If that works, I won't need you to use the blood."

"So, when are we staging this fight?"

"Tomorrow."

THICK CLOUDS of steam billow across the tile stone floor, fogging the clear glass that surrounds the shower. Too weak to stand, Jerrick sits on the stone bench and leans against the wall as water rains down on him.

He's been sitting like this for half an hour and knows he should get up. His back aches as he moves. Lathe did his best to heal him, but removing the dead, charred skin tissue was brutal, and he couldn't fix all the damage.

Once Lathe finished healing him, he helped him up to his third story room where Jerrick collapsed on his bed and slept like the dead for five hours. The throbbing ache in his back woke him and he was hoping the shower would relieve some of the discomfort, or at least loosen his tense muscles.

Jerrick forces himself to a stand, groaning with the movement. He uses the glass partition to steady himself as he exits the shower. He's toweling off when he hears the knock at his bedroom door.

He slips into sweats before opening the door.

Emily stands there, looking like she came straight from the war room. With teased windblown hair and skin brushed with ash, her emerald eyes shine with unshed tears. "My dad told me what happened. You're probably sick of my apologies by now, but I'm really sorry."

With his hand still wrapped around the knob, he moves to the side. "Come in." He steps away, moving to his dresser.

He freezes mid-movement when he feels her fingers run down the skin of his back, her voice as soft as her touch. "I did this to you."

He pulls open a drawer and grabs the shirt on top.

He winces when she places her palm flat over the center of his scar. "You're still in pain. Let me fix it."

She doesn't wait for permission. She dives right in. Lathe did an excellent job considering, but Jerrick feels Emily pushing herself to do more—to take away as much of the pain as possible.

"It's not necessary," he says, wasting his breath.

She heals what she can, which isn't much more than Lathe, but it allows him to stand straighter and untwists the scowl on his face. Once she's done, she drops her arm and steps back. "Is it true that Ashley once told you that you were every girl's wet dream?"

He pulls a shirt over his head and turns to face her. "Does that surprise you about her?"

Emily shrugs. "Not really. It's just . . . you seem so reserved. That had to make you uncomfortable."

"I don't know that Ashley means to share so many

thoughts out loud." He moves over to the end of his bed and takes a seat. "Sit." He pats the bed next to him.

She hesitates, staring at her feet before moving forward and taking a seat next to him. She sinks into the plush duvet, surprised such a masculine man has such a lavish bed.

"Evelyn chose you for a reason," he says.

She looks up at him. "Yeah, because she wanted me to lead the Olvasho."

"And free Latovia."

She shrugs, diverting her gaze. "I'm not sure I can."

Jerrick grins. "I don't think there's much you can't do. You stopped Sky, the reigning terror. You survived Adelaide, the evil queen, and Evelyn the tortured, confused soul. You've gone up against the most powerful Olvasho and you've won every time."

"But it's different fighting myself."

"Maybe you don't have to fight. You need to remove the burden from your younger self so you can continue on your journey. It might take time."

"Latovia doesn't have time."

After a beat of silence, Jerrick sighs. "I'm not here because you killed Sky. I know that's what Patrick said, but that's not the reason. It's not just your Valla blood that makes you special. You have courage, Emily. No one has faced the obstacles you have and come out the other side. I think Evelyn knew your potential. That's why she chose to visit you at four years old rather than going to your mother. I'm not speaking poorly of your mother, but from the little I know of her, she would not have handled things the way you have. I know you don't want to be a prophesy or our Vezetö, but it's not all about your power or your gifts. It's about the person carrying those burdens."

Emily is staring at the bedspread again, barely holding back tears.

Jerrick continues, "You love deeply, and it hurts you to see others suffer. You carry their pain with you until it becomes your pain, but I see it's killing you."

Emily sniffles, and Jerrick rocks up from the mattress with a groan. He grabs a tissue box from the bathroom and brings it to Emily before sitting beside her. "The things that happen in your memories are not your fault. You need to let go of the blame. You were too young to process it all. Your mind didn't know how to cope before, but now it does, so as you walk through your repressed memories, accept that you can't change the past, but acknowledge that it will help your future. Take the burdens from your five-year-old self. And then forgive yourself."

Emily blows her nose before looking up at him with a grin. "You make that sound easy."

"I know it won't be easy, but you wouldn't know what to do with something easy, anyway." He nudges her with his elbow. "It will be complicated, which you have more experience with. I think the real challenge is you have surpassed all the people you looked up to and now you feel lost."

INTRUDER

14

EMILY'S MOM guides her back through her memories. She woke up early this morning and has been at it for the last twelve hours. It's exhausting, but she knows she has to work on this until her psyche is better.

As she leaves a memory to move to the next, she feels a tug at her subconscious.

Patrick.

Patrick is talking about her.

She felt it—him talking about her.

He said her name.

The last time she revealed herself to him, he pushed her away. So, she wades in slowly, staying just out of his consciousness. She sees him—only him on a backdrop of white. He's talking to someone.

Who is he talking to?

She's plugged into his thoughts and feelings, and right now she feels his reluctance to believe what this person is telling him.

His voice comes to her crystal clear, and she realizes he's on the phone. She can't hear who he's on the phone with, but she feels the words being spoken through Patrick's mind. "You're saying she's created a second personality to protect herself?"

JERRICK FEELS he needs to keep Patrick current on the situation at the mansion, and so far, Patrick seemed willing to listen, until now.

Patrick scoffs, "You're saying she's created a second personality to protect herself?"

"I'm saying Evelyn traumatized her when she was little, and she didn't know how to handle it, so her mind found a way to escape the trauma."

"By going into the fugue state," Patrick asks. "So essentially, she created a second personality who thinks she's five?"

Jerrick switches the phone to his other ear, his body stiff and aching. "Not exactly. I'm saying that when she enters this fugue state, she reverts back to her five-year-old self."

"Are you trying to tell me a five-year-old tortured us?"

Jerrick rolls his neck. "Not at all. When she was five, she didn't have the power she has now, so her five-year-old self is scared, misplaced, and can't comprehend the magic she possesses. Basically, the power of her blood takes over to protect her and she becomes raw protective magic, using any means necessary to defend her inner child. That is what tortured us."

"So how do we get rid of it?" Patrick asks.

"We can't," he says, stretching an arm across his chest. "It only goes away when Emily's mind feels rested, and she wakes on her own, or when five-year-old Emily feels safe, like when she saw Mark because her younger self recognized him as someone safe. Right now, she's working through the repressed memories, but it might take time. She's seen some very disturbing things. The trauma is real." He pauses, switching the phone to his other hand so he can stretch the other arm. "Speaking of which, there is something she saw that relates to you."

"Oh, yeah. And what's that?"

Jerrick lets go of the stretch and releases a breath. "She had memories of you at a hotel in Chicago when you were young. It was brief, but she saw your whole life flash through her mind. Well, everything up to a certain point. The vision was graphic, and she's feeling guilty for not stopping it, but it's not her fault."

PATRICK RUNS a hand through his hair and sighs. "I have to go. I have someone waiting on me, and I don't know what I'm supposed to say to all of this anyway."

Emily wants to know who's waiting on him. After he hangs up, she can see Patrick moving across the blank white space. He opens a door she can't see, and the background noise fills her mind. Patrick has a seat across from someone, a woman. Emily can't see her, but she feels his attraction.

"Sorry about that," he says.

The woman's voice echoes in Patrick's mind, "Important call?"

"I thought so, but as it turns out, it was a waste of time."

She laughs and her hand strokes his arm, which sends a volt of temptation through him. "Patrick, I'm so happy I met you. I was beginning to think good men no longer existed."

Patrick chuckles. It's a fake laugh, and Emily hates it. "I don't know that I'm a good man. I just couldn't leave you stranded."

"No one else stopped to help. Only you. How are you single?"

Emily waits for his answer with bated breath.

"Truth is, I just got out of a complicated relationship."

This time her hand lands on his thigh. "I hear that. My ex was a disaster, but I promise you, I'm not complicated."

Emily smirks as she feels Patrick's desire wane. He doesn't do simple relationships. Although, he had flings that were uncomplicated.

"I'm not looking for a serious relationship right now. I've still got some items to work out."

His mind registers her hand rubbing his thigh. Emily feels his reaction to her touch and knows about his growing arousal. Even though she knows she should retreat out of his mind, she stays, needing to know what happens next. Needing to see how far he lets this go.

PATRICK FEELS HER PRESENCE. He knows she's there, lurking in the recesses of his mind and it pisses him off. She's not giving him the one thing he asked for: space. So, if she wants to misinterpret what's happening here, then that's fine. But he will not make it easy for her.

He stopped to help someone with a flat tire. It hardly makes him a hero, but the thankful woman asked to buy him dinner. He only agreed because Morgan was out tonight, and he didn't want to be alone. But should anyone ask, it's because he hasn't interacted with people who don't know his secret in quite some time. This was practice.

So here he is, sitting across from a beautiful, slightly desperate woman. He isn't really interested in her, but then he felt Emily watching from his subconscious, like she was peeking through the window on a private moment. So, if this beautiful woman wants to take him home and get frisky, it's not like he is tied down, and it would serve Emily right for violating his privacy.

He shifts in his seat, spreading his thighs to give her better access. Not that he thinks she'll do anything but light petting down here, but he knows she lives in one of the apartments above the bar.

Patrick looks around the bar. "I love old buildings. They have so much character. This place must be historic."

She grins a seductive grin. "It is. I have an apartment upstairs, and the hardwood is original. It's what made me fall in love with the place."

"So much history."

"Would you like to see it?"

There it is.

He gives her a lazy grin. "I would love to."

They have already paid for their drinks, so she stands, and he follows her out. They leave the bar and go to a side entrance where they climb the stairs to her apartment.

EMILY KNOWS she should separate herself, but it's too horrible not to witness with her own eyes. The woman gives Patrick a tour through the apartment which ends in her bedroom. Her boobs press against his chest, and her hands play in his hair. They are close enough to kiss, but neither of them has made a move.

"I know we just met, Patrick, but I feel you want to kiss me just as much as I want to kiss you."

Emily scoffs. "Yeah, if kiss means fuck."

Shit. She knows she just gave herself away. There is no way Patrick didn't hear her.

After a brief pause, he says to the woman. "Why stop at kissing."

She laughs and her lips lift to his.

Emily fights to leave his consciousness, but she's too upset to think clearly, which only keeps her there longer—long enough for his new girl to unbuckle his pants.

Then she's out—out of his head, but still caught in the tornado of her own mind. Her power coils and zaps at her subconscious until she lets it out with a scream. Fire bursts from her.

She knows she's in the war room. It can take the heat and wrath of her anger.

The others will assume that her magic has taken over, but she's controlling this energy, forcing it out until she feels empty—until she won't have to try so hard every second of every day.

Only she realizes something else. Her power has grown. She hadn't realized her magic was tangled and snagged on all the things she had repressed. By exposing her repressed memories and dealing with them, she has untangled her magic from the web of her own making. The ease in which she wields her power is incredible, but she knows it could be even better. Now that she is aware of the snags, she can spot the few remaining knots.

She extinguishes the fire and falls back inward to repair herself.

QUIVERS

15

Deja exits the portal behind Ashley. Lathe is waiting in the underground tunnel, and Deja averts her eyes, still angry with him. She crosses her arms and goes to wait by the elevator while Ashley goes to Lathe. The couple embraces, whispering secrets to each other. Deja rolls her eyes and taps her fingers against her arm.

Ashley uncurls her arms from around Lathe's neck as she steps back, her hands tentative on his arms as her voice gets loud. "What is that supposed to mean?"

He scoffs. "What do you want me to say, Ashley? I can't make promises. I don't know if we can free Latovia, and even if we can, you're his wife and their queen."

"Because of you!" She backs further until her arms are at her sides, and the distance between them may as well be a canyon. "You're the one who introduced me to him and Latovia. If it hadn't been for that, then maybe I would've had a chance at a normal life."

Lathe leans against the arm of the sofa behind him, his eyes averted. "I don't want to argue."

She throws her hands out. "You always want to argue. Arguing shows passion and passion is good, right?"

"Passion is like a candle. It burns hot and heavy, but once the candle melts, the fire stops burning, and you're left with nothing but a useless mess."

Her forehead pulls tight as she steps away. "You think I'm a useless mess?"

Deja steps forward, wondering if their staged fight might become real. "Ashley?"

Ashley looks to Deja, standing by the elevator. "He's not the reason we came."

"Right," Ashley says with resolution, walking toward the elevator. "Let's go."

"Wait." Lathe pushes off the couch, and Ashley starts to turn when he says, "Deja, I need to talk to you."

Deja scowls at him. "No thanks." She hits the button for the elevator and the doors ding open.

"Deja," he says more demanding.

She turns to him, snapping, "What?"

Ashley steps on the elevator, waiting for her.

Lathe's eyes narrow on her, not aggressively, but like he's looking too closely, and she hesitates.

Glancing toward Ashley, Deja says, "Go on without me. I'll meet you in Latovia."

Ashley nods, and the door closes between them. Deja steps forward. "What? You're talking to me now."

"Her skin is changing too quickly, and she keeps reassuring me that it's fine, but I won't be the reason she dies."

"Why are you telling me?"

"I'm trying to explain why I was so irrational the other night. I'm sorry." His eyes give her a look that tells her he's sorry.

She scowls. "Grownups are confusing."

He makes a face. "Something's bothering you."

Deja's brows shoot up. "What?"

"What is it?"

She shrugs and he moves forward. "Deja, Seriously, what is it?"

"My friend is missing. A few orphans are."

Lathe pales. "Does Wolfe know?"

She swallows. "I'll tell him when we get back."

"Why not go tell him now?"

"Ashley asked me to come with her."

"I'll deal with Ashley. You go help your friend," he says with enough force that she doesn't argue.

She nods. "Thanks, Lathe," she says before going through the portal.

Latovia is quiet when she arrives. She takes the shortcut, running all the way to Wolfe's chambers. When she arrives, Wolfe is looking at the maps sprawled across his desk. She interrupts, panting, "Lathe and Ashley just staged a pretty convincing fight in front of me. They don't trust you."

He glances at her. "Or you, if they didn't let you into their plan."

Deja comes forward. "I think she's going to make a move on you."

"What makes you think that?"

"You're her husband." She shrugs. "It makes sense."

He shakes his head, looking at the maps. "I hope you're wrong."

"Me too."

"Thanks, Deja," he says, dismissing her.

She steps closer, her hands resting tentatively on the desk. "What is your move, Wolfe? We have to work with them if we want out of here, so why are you holding back?"

Only his eyes shift to her, and his gruff voice lowers. "They are already hesitant of our powers. If they knew the truth, they'd never risk saving us."

Deja swallows. "But people are dying."

He pounds his fist on the desk. "Because they are breaking the laws!"

She takes a shaky breath. "Because they've lost faith in you."

His whole body turns toward her in warning. "I'm still your king."

She averts her eyes, confessing, "Orphans are missing."

"How long?"

Looking at her worn-out shoes, she says, "A day."

"That could be nothing."

"I've heard the rumors about roaming blood magic."

"I've taught you better than to listen to rumors," he scoffs.

"You taught me to be curious and careful." She looks up at him. "I can't be both. If I get too curious around wild magic, you'll have one more missing orphan kid."

Wolfe runs a hand over his face and his shoulders slump. "Everything has become so unstable. The magic keeps shifting, but it's more active at night, so I'll deal with it tonight." He looks back down at the map, dismissing her.

ASHLEY KISSES LATHE. "Do you think she bought our fight?"

"I think she's preoccupied. Orphans have gone missing."

"Shit." Ashley steps back. "When? Does Wolfe know?"

"She just went to tell him."

"Okay." Her brows fall together. "Why didn't she tell me?"

"Deja is a hard nut to crack. I've known her longer than you have."

Ashley shakes her head. "You're right. Okay. I'd better get back there then. If I'm not back in a few hours, come to Latovia."

"I will." He gives her another kiss before she goes through the portal.

Ashley walks toward Wolfe's chambers. Her pace quickening at the sudden unease. The fine hair on the back of her neck rises just before the whispers begin. She can't understand the muttered words, but she understands their meaning. Dragons.

She's practically running by the time she reaches the chamber door. She forces herself to slow down and take a breath before entering.

It's dark when she enters, and that creepy unease returns. "Wolfe?"

After no response, she moves to the side room, but it appears just as dark. "Wolfe? What's going on?"

The main chamber door opens, and all the gems return to their golden glow as Wolfe walks into the room.

Ashley steps out from the side room. "Why was it dark in here?"

Wolfe looks surprised to see her. "We've been getting weird magic surges all day."

"I've never seen the gems glow navy."

"It happens sometimes," he says with a shrug.

She wants to question him further, but she won't gain his trust by giving him the third degree, so she says, "It was kind of beautiful. It reminded me of the night sky."

Wolfe watches her from across the room. "Did you get the books I asked for?"

She spins the bag around on her shoulder and pulls out two books before leaving the bag on the hook with the coats. "I've gotta say, you have an eclectic taste in books. First seismology and now physics and origins of magic." They meet in the middle of the room.

He takes the books, asking, "How are things going with Emily?"

"Sounds like she's making progress."

"Good." He nods.

"Lathe and I got in a fight."

Wolfe lifts his brows. "Deja mentioned that." He turns and moves to the desk.

"He makes me so angry. He thinks I should stop visiting him."

Wolfe sets the books on the desk and leans back against it. "I'm assuming you laughed in his face."

"No." She scoffs. "I don't do well with rejection. I'm not disposable. I'm a princess for god sakes."

"Actually, you're a queen."

She rolls her eyes. "He reminded me of that, too. He said I should just be with you, that it would make more sense."

"It would make more sense if we didn't want to kill each other eighty percent of the time."

Ashley steps forward. "But maybe that's just sexual tension."

He laughs.

Ashley doesn't. She takes another step, placing herself right in front of him. His arms are at his sides, his hands spread out on the edge of the desk. She stares at him as she places her hand against his chest.

He's smirking at her like he finds this all too funny.

Ashley bites her lip at the same time she releases a hint of her magic against his chest. She watches the current spread outward like an electrical web until the tiny surge dissipates.

His smirk dies, and he looks down at the palm against his chest. He pulls her hand away and his fingers lace through hers. Before she comprehends what he's doing, she feels the sparks of his magic sizzle up her arm and travel through her body.

"Holy shit," she mumbles, looking up at him with surprise. His eyes have the smallest ring of blue encircling them, reflecting his magic. Wolfe rarely showed his magic, and she assumed it's because he barely had any, but as she feels it trickle through her, she realizes how wrong she was.

She pulls out of his grip, losing track of what she's supposed to be doing.

Clasping her hands together over her chest, she watches Wolfe's grin spread. She's not used to his smile. She hadn't known she could be attracted to him. He was always too authoritative and cold, but she has never seen this side of him.

He's without his dragon skin jacket, and she looks at the tattoos on his arms, the black ink barely darker than his skin. She reaches out, her fingers brushing over the Latovian marriage symbol on his left arm. She jerks her hand away when it lights up, glowing purple.

"It recognizes you," he whispers. "The gems they add to the ink is filled with your magic. Just like your tattoo is filled with my magic." He pulls up her sleeve, and his fingers brush the inside of her arm. The tattoo glows with navy light. The same color the stones were glowing when she walked in here.

"Why do you hide your magic?" she asks him, still staring at her arm where the navy bands continue to glow.

"I don't want my people to fear me. I want them to respect me."

His hand gently tilts her chin up to him, as he asks, "Do you respect me, Ashley?"

This is her opening. Her eyes meet his before flicking to his lips. "I do. More each day." Her hand grazes over his tattoo again as it slides up his arm, before abandoning his bicep for a lock of hair. His dreadlocks come down to mid-chest and are always impeccably well-groomed. She twirls a lock around her finger and tugs playfully at it as she leans against him.

One of his arms meets the small of her back as he asks, "What are you doing, princess?"

She lifts onto her toes and whispers against his mouth. "I don't know."

"You sure this is the move you want to make?"

"I'm not sure about anything, anymore," she says before pressing her lips to his. They're softer than she expected.

His grip on her tightens as his hands slide up her body as he returns her kiss.

Ashley thinks she has him right where she wants him until she feels the tingle of magic where his hand meets the skin of her neck. Her legs weaken along with her resolve.

Her hands grip his shoulders, wrapping around his neck as desire flares and their tongues meet. Their magic mingles, and it's like nothing she's ever experienced. He grips her ass and picks her up, sitting her on the desk.

She pulls back, panting, needing to catch her breath, but he holds her tighter. His breath against her neck sends a shiver down her spine. His teeth nibble her ear, and he tugs her to the edge of the desk, pressing into her. "You're so full of shit, sunshine," he whispers, as his obvious arousal grinds against her. She gasps as he uses Lathe's nickname for her, but she can't go anywhere.

"Lathe wouldn't hurt you." His hands glide up her back, his magic overwhelming her with need. His breath at her ear has her pressing into him—her back arching and her chest rubbing against his as he lays her back against the desk. "He wouldn't hurt you." He bites at her ear until it hurts. "But I would."

He pulls away all at once, leaving her sprawled on his desk. Her hand goes to her ear as she stares up at the gem covered ceiling in a daze, only realizing he left the room when she hears the door close.

After regaining some sense, Ashley rolls off the desk, and in a huff, she storms into his chambers without knocking, demanding, "What the hell was that?"

Wolfe is undressing, leaving his chest exposed as he bends down to remove his boots.

She stops just inside the door, gasping, "What are you doing?"

"I'm changing."

"Why?"

He glances at her. "Because we have wild magic loose in Latovia and it's our job to go look for it. I'm not wearing lounge clothes out to do that."

"Those are your lounge clothes? They all look the same." She looks away when he pulls down his pants with nothing underneath. "Whoa."

"You're the one who walked into my bedroom."

"Yes, but can you stop while we're talking?"

"Fine."

She looks back at him, and he's standing completely naked, waiting for her to continue.

She sighs and turns away, trying not to get his body stuck in her memory. "My ear is bleeding where you bit me like a fucking savage."

Suddenly his hand is at her ear. His fingers run down it, and she feels the graze of magic before he pulls away. When she reaches up, it's healed.

She hears him moving about the room and wants to yell at him for what just happened, but doesn't know where to begin.

She only finds out that he's dressed when he walks past her and out the door.

She follows him out, saying, "How dare you—"

He spins on her before the second word is out of her mouth and steps in close, his voice low. "How dare I? You're the one who put on a whole little production. Your little fight with Lathe, you coming to me for what, comfort, reassurance?" He scoffs. "Because I'm the guy you go to for those things. How dumb do you think I am?"

"I just wanted you to trust me."

He gives her a look of bewilderment. "How would any of that make me trust you?"

Her words are soft. "I thought if we were closer, you would trust me with all of Latovia's secrets."

"I have told you everything I can about Latovia, and I have been so patient with you. And the way you went about this was despicable. Do you think no one has tried to seduce me before? The first woman I took to my bed tried to murder me in my sleep. I killed her instead. Sex isn't about love. It's about power, and there might be Latovians who will fight to the death to get a piece of you, but I'm not one of them. Not because you aren't pretty, or because you don't do it for me, but because you undermine me at every turn."

"Because you're lying to me!" she cries.

"Oh, right. About the dragons. I don't know how to get it through your thick skull. The dragons are a figment of your overactive, overdramatic, imagination." He sighs. "You have to trust me instead of acting like a child who gets mad at mommy when she tells you not to play in the street. You might not see the car coming, but I do, and there I am jumping in front of the fucking car just so you don't die. Now, stop asking about dragons," he warns, looming over her. "You're implanting the idea into people's minds, and if enough Latovian people believe in dragons, guess what will happen?"

She presses her lips together with a scowl. "It could make dragons real?"

He nods, "And not the kind we knew and could trust, but dragons made from wildly unstable blood magic. Blood magic we can't always contain or control. Believing in a portal door killed two people, imagine the harm a warped dragon could have on Latovia."

Ashley's face changes and her head comes up. "So, you're saying it's possible to create a dragon, one that is all fucked up and maybe feeds off children?"

Wolfe straightens. "Deja said orphans were missing."

"So maybe the people already believe in dragons."

Wolfe walks to his desk. "Go get Deja. I want to see what she knows."

"Do you know where she is?"

He shrugs. "Her usual places."

"Why aren't you coming with me?"

He picks up one of the new books she brought him. "I have a book to skim."

"Fine," she sighs, leaving through the double doors. She looks at her watch. She has an hour before Lathe comes, and she thinks about calling it off, but first, she needs to find Deja.

As soon as the double door closes, Wolfe sets the book down, saying, "You can come out."

Deja steps out of the side room, moving toward him with a scowl.

"How long have you been there?"

"Long enough," she snips.

He sees her look. "What?"

"I think they would understand."

Wolfe's gruff laughter fills the room. "Being the king of people with failing magic differs from being the king of dragons."

"I think they would understand," she repeats, her big eyes on him.

They stare at one another for a silent moment before he steps back from the desk. "Deja, turn around and close your eyes."

She quickly turns around and squeezes her eyes shut. The sound of stones grinding and crumbling causes Deja to cover her head and duck, but nothing hits her. The cave vibrates around them, the trembling so strong, her eyes fly open and she spins around, sure she's about to be crushed.

She gasps, her body forgetting how to move as glowing red eyes stare at her from the ceiling where the creature is crawling across solid stone. Then the lights go dim, all the gold gems replaced by a dark navy glow.

"Wolfe?" She hates the quiver in her voice. She's supposed to be fearless, but she's never seen something so terrifying, and now she can't tell where it is or what's going on. Everything is just shadows.

Wolfe's voice comes from right next to her. "You still think I should tell the Olvasho? You think they will help us?"

She's shaking her head. "No. I . . . Wolfe, where is it?" She spins, her lip quivering as tears burn in her eyes.

"He's gone." As he says it, the gem's golden light returns.

Her chest rises and falls as she tries to catch her breath. "That's what they look like?"

"More or less," he says, sounding matter of fact.

She's always trusted Wolfe. He's been like a brother since her parent's died. She's never doubted him, but now she's beginning to.

"Let's go find Ashley," he says, slipping into his jacket and grabbing the long one from Ashley's hook.

WILD

16

"Ashley!" Deja's voice echoes down the cavern.

Ashley spins, seeing Deja and Wolfe walking towards her. As they meet up, Wolfe says, "Wild magic was spotted by Rainbow Falls." He holds out a jacket to her. "It's a hike. Do you need to change your shoes?"

She slips into the long dragon skin jacket. "I'm good."

Wolfe turns to Deja. "You keep a lookout here."

Deja nods before turning away.

Wolfe jerks his head to the side. "This way."

They walk in silence for the next half-hour until Ashley can no longer stand it. "Latovia is too big for walking. You need horses down here or something."

"We tried that once. The mess and smell weren't worth it. They were delicious, though."

Her mouth falls open. "You ate horses?"

"Oh, that horrifies you, but the thought of us skinning our dragon didn't bother you?"

Ashley shrugs. "Are there animals in Latovia? Besides the chickens."

"There are goats and pigs because they're not as picky with their food, but we have them tucked away. It's a forty-five-minute walk just to get there from the main cavern, and it's not a pleasant trip."

"Why'd you let me come on to you if you knew what I was doing?" Ashley asks in a sudden topic change.

He sighs. "Curiosity. I wondered how far you'd go, and I've questioned what Lathe sees in you. I thought maybe you were just really skilled at sex."

"Well, according to you, it's all about power. Did I at least live up to the hype?"

He glances at her with a shrug. "We didn't have sex."

"Yeah, but. . ."

"But what?" he asks with a raised brow.

With a scowl, she admits, "But that was good, right? Like that magic, I've just never—"

"Oh. You're talking about the mating-meld, when magic intermingles."

"Mating-meld. Sounds made up."

"I guess I just assumed you and Lathe had . . . Guess not."

"I didn't know it was possible."

"But you initiated it."

"Yeah, but I didn't know what I was actually like doing. I just somehow knew that would get you to stop laughing."

"Maybe you're succumbing to our Latovian ways."

"Maybe." She shrugs. "I'm definitely trying that magic melding thing with Lathe."

"You sure he'll want you after you came on to me."

"Oh, he'll be pissed, but it won't be at me. And he knows I was trying to earn your trust. He just didn't know how," she says as they approach the rainbow falls.

She pulls her engagement ring out of her pocket, slips it on her finger, and holds it up. "He proposed yesterday."

Wolfe glances at it. "It's Latovian."

"Yep. His grandfather proposed to his grandmother with this ring. It's kismet. They were a Latolvasho couple who fell in love and so are we."

"Latolvasho?"

"Yeah he was Latovian and she was Olvasho. Latolvasho."

Wolfe grimaces, shaking his head. "Stop trying to create words."

The sound of the falls echoing in the cavern fills the next stretch of silence between them as they stare at the cascading water.

With hundreds of Latovian gems on the cliff behind the falls, it used to be full of color, making the water look like a rainbow, but now it's mostly gold with a few specks of purple.

Looking down at the falls, Ashley says, "You should add some navy gems."

He glances at her. "Do you think Lathe will ever risk coming here?"

"You mean when the curse is broken?"

"No, I mean now. He's a fourth Latovian. His mom was only half Latovian and look what she did for Latovia."

She's already shaking her head. "Lathe has power, but it feels totally different from Evelyn's. And don't think I don't know you changed the subject on purpose. Make some navy gems."

"No, we're working."

"Really?" she questions. "Do you feel wild magic because I sure as heck don't."

He lets out a big breath. "No, but maybe it's dormant, waiting for us to leave."

"You think it knows we're here?"

"Or maybe it just hasn't come out for the night."

Ashley looks down at her watch. "It's almost midnight."

"Fine, let's head back."

LATHE SITS on the edge of the couch, leg bouncing in anticipation. He's hoping she comes through the portal door. His finger taps against his leg. Ashley is smart—smarter than people give her credit. She wouldn't ask him to come unless she needed him and knew he wouldn't die instantly upon entering.

She is absolutely certain there are dragons, and he's not sure what to do if he doesn't hear what she hears. He sighs, looking at the clock. Only five minutes until midnight. She wouldn't cut it this close. He stands, going to stand in front of the new mirror he added for this very purpose. Stripping down to only his boxers, he lets out a big sigh before opening the bag that contains the jar of blood.

He unscrews the lid, and even after storing it in the refrigerator, the iron smell is horrendous. Skin crawling, he sticks his hand in the blood and smears it down his arm,

trying not to think about the dead Latovian man who invol-
untarily donated to their cause.

He cakes it on, down each leg, across his torso, over his
face. Once he's covered every inch, he waits for it to dry a
little before pulling on a long dragon skin jacket Ashley had
gifted him. He slips into some boots and takes one last look
in the mirror.

It's time for him to go through. He doesn't like this, but
he shoves aside his reservations and moves to the portal door.

WOLFE HAD a few ideas where they may find the wild
magic, but so far, they'd come across nothing but rock and
the occasional Latovian.

"It's already midnight," Ashley complains. "From what
you said, the magic should be running wild by now."

There is a burst of magic, and they both pause in their
step. "Did you feel that?"

"Yeah," Ashley glances in the direction of the portal
door. Lathe is right on time.

"I'm not sure which direction, though. Should we split
up?" Ashley suggests. "If I find it, I'll send out a flare of
magic so you can find me."

Wolfe nods, "But you're taking Deja with you. She's
more familiar with these caves than you are."

Ashley rolls her eyes, trying to look irritated instead of
angry that he's thwarted her plans.

They rush toward the royal chambers to a notch high in
the wall where Deja had taken to sleeping. "I don't like that
she sleeps here alone," Ashley notes.

"She said it's more centralized so she can get places faster, and it gives her warning if someone tries to sneak up on her."

"She's eight. She shouldn't have to worry about someone sneaking up on her."

Wolfe shrugs. "Should or shouldn't. It's her reality."

"So why don't you invite her to stay in the royal chambers. I have my own room. She could stay with me."

Wolfe shakes his head. "She won't. I've tried."

"You're the king. You can make her."

His eyes flick to her, and he growls, "Choice is the only real thing that hasn't been taken from her. I won't take her choice in exchange for safety, but she knows there will always be a place for her."

"She's eight! She doesn't know what's best for her."

He shakes his head. "Just because your mom made your choices for you for most of your life, doesn't mean you can make Deja's."

Ashley glares at him. "You're a dick. I'll find my own way."

She turns and walks away from him, going to find Lathe.

WOLFE WATCHES HER WALK AWAY, purposefully pissing her off to get her out of harm's way. He knows exactly where the magic burst came from, so he let her go off in the opposite direction.

"Deja!" he shouts.

Her head pops out of a notch in the wall about ten feet from where they had argued.

"Deja, will you keep an eye on Ashley. Keep her to the west, around the portal to Lathe's. The magic is in the south-eastern corner. Can you do that for me?"

"Of course." She crawls out of the hole in the wall and scales down the rock like a pro. Her feet touch down, and she notices he's staring at her shoes.

"Why didn't you tell me you need new shoes?"

"These are fine."

"Those have holes in them."

"Ashley already gave me a new pair, but they're too loud."

"I don't have time to argue. Just keep Ashley safe," he says before taking off in a jog.

Before Ashley can reach the portal door, Deja catches up to her. "Hold up. I'm supposed to make sure you don't get lost."

Ashley rolls her eyes, having the urge to call her Wolfe's lapdog, but she doesn't want to offend Deja, she wants to hurt Wolfe for being so unpleasant.

There is another burst of magic that rocks through Ashley, and she pauses, almost tripping mid-step. "What the hell?"

Deja stops beside her. "Is it magic? Where?"

She wants to answer, but she can't as the magic seems to be everywhere and nowhere. She runs forward as the hair at the back of her neck stands on end, and goosebumps rise all over her body.

She feels Lathe. He's somewhere close, but when she

reaches the portal door, she doesn't see him. He couldn't have gone far.

Deja catches up to Ashley. "What was that?"

An explosion of wild magic rocks through her, and the cave shakes beneath her feet. Deja grabs onto Ashley. "Ashley, what is happening?"

"I don't know," she says as the whispers start in her ear. "Do you hear that?"

"Hear what?"

"Whispering?"

"I don't hear anything."

Ashley takes off in a direction, trying to latch on to Lathe's aura. It's faint, but she follows with Deja as her shadow.

She freezes. "Deja, stay right where you are."

She peeks around the corner to find Lathe.

LATHE CAN'T JUST STAND by the portal door covered in Latovian blood. He has to find somewhere a little less conspicuous, but somewhere Ashley can still locate him. He goes down a tunnel and hides behind a dead-end notch in the cavern wall.

He stays hidden until he hears Deja's voice echoing down the tunnel, "Hear what?"

"Whispering?" Ashley says.

"I don't hear anything."

Lathe does, and it keeps getting louder. Whispers he can't make out—whispers of a hundred people all at once—a cacophony of voices in such a quiet noise. Chills spread across his skin, and he steps out of his hiding spot, trying to follow Ashley's voice. And then he hears her plain as day. "Deja, stay right where you are."

Ashley steps around the corner, only thirty feet away. She makes eye contact with him, her eyes wide and her face as pale as her corpse had been. He's never seen her look so scared—not when his mother killed her—not when his mother died. Never.

She swallows as she steps forward. Her eyes flick to the ground between them. He was so caught up on watching her; he didn't notice the magic moving toward him like fog spreading across a graveyard.

He looks behind him, realizing there is nowhere for him to run. He'd backed himself in a corner. His eyes lift to hers, and she steps forward.

He shakes his head. "It's okay."

"We can fight it," she says.

He shakes his head, feeling the potent wild magic. "My power is weak here. There is no fighting this." He steps back. "You should run."

"No," she whispers, shaking her head as she sniffles. She looks back at the magic, and her jaw grows hard as her teeth clench. Her top lip curls into a growl. "I said, no!"

Lathe watches her eyes shine like purple gems, and her spine arches as her feet leave the ground. Her head shoots back.

"RUN!" She shouts, her voice echoing across the cavern as the magic fog flips direction, spinning toward Ashley. It goes after her with the speed of a tornado, wrapping its hazy arms around her until all he can see is a twirling purple fog.

Lathe runs toward her. "Ashley!"

Deja runs around the corner just as the twirling purple magic disappears through the cave wall with Ashley. Lathe grabs hold of his weakened abilities to blow a hole clean through the dense rock. As stones fall, and the ground rumbles, dust fills the air so thick that both he and Deja choke on it.

Lathe clears the air with a forceful breeze and runs through the hole he created. It leads to another cavern tunnel, but he doesn't see Ashley or the pool of wild magic.

He brings his arms back, ready to knock through another wall, but Deja grabs his arms, hanging on with all her weight.

"No, Lathe! Stop!"

He tries to shake her off.

"She's gone, Lathe! You won't find her by knocking down walls, and Latovia is already collapsing. You could hurt someone."

"She's not gone!"

"You won't find her this way."

The sound of thunder rumbles through the cave from the other direction, and Lathe turns to Deja in question.

Deja's frantic gaze sweeps the space, landing on him. "Shit!" She grabs his hand. "Come on!"

She takes off at a run.

He goes along with her, complaining, "Are you taking me to Wolfe?"

"No. I'm getting you out of here."

"But . . . Ashley."

"It would've taken her if you were here or not, but we need to get you out of here before Wolfe kills you."

He pulls against her hold. "Deja, I can't leave without doing something."

"You are doing something. You're protecting yourself."

"Deja."

"I can't lose you!" she shouts, tears coming to her eyes. "Don't ask me to lose you too!"

He kneels down, and she pushes against him, fighting his sympathetic gaze. "We have to leave," she cries.

He shakes his head. "I need to talk to Wolfe."

She is shaking her head before he can complete his sentence. "No. Wolfe will kill us." Her nostrils flare and her eyes shine with tears.

His gaze narrows as he stands. "Why?"

Deja runs her hands down her face before making fists. "Wolfe sent me to distract her. I was supposed to lead Ashley away from the magic, and I failed. Now the magic has Ashley, and it's my fault."

"Wolfe would never hurt you, and we'll find Ashley."

She shakes her head again and starts tugging him toward the portal door. "I'm not listening to you. You're covered in Latovian blood like some kind of idiot that wants to start a war!" She tugs at him again. "Come on."

He relents, but as they step forward, all the purple and gold gems illuminating their way go dark, replaced by a midnight navy glow, so dim, they can't see but a few feet in any direction.

Deja's voice shakes as she breathes a warning. "Wolfe." Her trembling hand squeezes Lathe's.

Lathe tries to block her from harm, but he can't tell where his opponent lies. He spins, barely able to make out the surrounding shadows.

Lathe feels a whoosh of cool air against his face, and he places Deja behind him just as Wolfe's gruff voice fills the cavern. It's everywhere—all-consuming, leaving no trace of direction to pinpoint a location.

"Why did you cover yourself in Latovian blood?" the voice booms.

Lathe swallows, searching the darkness. "Why are you hiding, Wolfe?"

"It is a myth that covering yourself in Latovian blood will protect you from the curse."

Lathe shrugs. "It's working."

"No. Your grandfather's blood is protecting you. The blood you're wearing is offensive."

Deja pulls Lathe toward the cavern wall, but he's reluctant. "The magic wrapped itself around Ashley and—"

"I'll take care of Ashley," Wolfe's cuts him off, "but you have to leave. You're a diversion, and you're tearing down walls in my kingdom. Don't come back here. You can't break the curse. You can't help us here. It was Valla blood that placed the spell, so it is Valla blood that will break it. If you want to save Ashley, then fix Emily."

"Why won't you show yourself?"

A gust of wind hits Lathe, and he hears a rustling.

"Get Emily to break the curse!"

A second later, the gems transform, shining bright purple and gold, and Wolfe is nowhere to be seen. Lathe turns to Deja for an explanation.

She tugs his arm, getting him safely through the portal door. Her eyes widen as she asks, "You and Wolfe were talking?"

"Yes."

She shakes her head. "Don't go back, Lathe. You can't ever go back to Latovia."

"I've never seen you look afraid of him."

"Latovians are dangerous." She breathes heavily, swiping at her tears before they fall. "I don't want to die," she whimpers, "but you shouldn't free us. You shouldn't trust us." Unable to hold back, she sobs in earnest. Lathe pulls her close, hugging her as tears fall.

ONCE UPON A KALEIDOSCOPE

17

EMILY PUSHES through each barrier of her memory, feeling like she'd been at this for days, even though it had only been hours since she snuck into Patrick's mind and witnessed him with another woman. She's glad she saw it. It's what sparked her angry burst of magic—a power stronger than she had ever felt. And she realized her magic had been coiled up inside her, hidden within repressed memories.

Now she'd gone back through her remaining memories, feeling grief and freedom with each as she lets go of the guilt she hadn't realized she was holding. Now she needs to face her younger self, finally putting her inner child at peace.

Emily walks down a white hall in her mind. It looks just like the hall at her preschool, which is where her younger mind probably conjured the image. Emily strides toward the double doors at the end of the sterile smelling corridor. She pushes through the doors and feels warmth inside the room filled with bright colors and tiny desks. A road creates a path through the town on the carpet, while bins labeled with familiar names fill the red cubbies on the wall. The familiar space reminds her of simpler times, bringing with it a sense of peace.

A lone girl sits on the floor playing with dolls, but she looks up when Emily arrives, and the toys around her disappear. The little girl stands as Emily approaches.

"Hello," Emily says.

"Hi," her inner child responds.

"How old are you?"

"Four. No, six." She looks at Emily with confusion. "I can't remember."

"But you are the younger me?"

The girl smirks. "I came first, so I think that makes you the older me."

Emily smiles. "Thank you for protecting me. You don't have to do it anymore."

Her inner-self says, "But I don't want to die."

"You'll always be a part of me."

She bites her lip, looking less at peace. "But I don't want you to die either."

Emily tilts her head in question as the little girl turns toward a toy chest. She digs through, pulling out a silver and pink tube. She holds it out.

"A kaleidoscope?" Emily questions, taking the offered toy.

"Sort of." Her inner child backs away. "I was hiding it to protect us. It's the last memory."

"Thank you." Emily hugs her inner child before closing one eye to peer into the kaleidoscope. The internal reflective surfaces create patterns of overlapping colors before the designs become too complex for a child's toy, and it submerges her into a memory—no, a vision—a prophetic vision of her death. *Her last memory.*

Fire rains down from the heavens as winged demons fly through the night sky, exhaling flames. The mansion and stables burn while frightened horses run wild across the vast landscape.

ALEC SITS UP IN BED, awakened by her screams. He looks around, feeling the spot where Morgan had fallen asleep. She isn't there. He gets out of bed and searches for her. It's one in the morning. She must have left after he fell asleep. He sends her a text which goes unanswered.

As he gets dressed, he can't help but feel a growing panic in his chest. Something is wrong. He swears he heard her scream. He pulls his phone back out and calls Morgan, but her phone goes to voicemail.

He's already getting in his car before he thinks to call Patrick, so he calls him on his drive over.

"Hello," Patrick's groggy voice answers.

"Did Morgan get home?"

Patrick pauses. "Yeah, she's here."

Patrick's reassurance does nothing to calm Alec.

When Alec doesn't respond, Patrick asks, "Alec, what's happening?"

"Will you check on her?"

"Why are you freaking out?"

"Never mind, I'm on my way over." Alec hangs up before Patrick can object.

When Alec arrives, he uses his key to enter and goes

straight to Morgan's bedroom, finding her sitting on the edge of her bed, yawning.

Her presence is a cooling balm and before she can finish questioning what he's doing there, he has his arms wrapped around her.

She returns his embrace. "Alec, what's going on?"

"I don't know. I just needed to see you." Despite having Morgan safe in his arms, the panic seeps back in.

"Are you having nightmares again?" Her voice is soft.

"No, I don't think so. This felt different. I woke up to you screaming."

"Are you sure it was me? Did you check on your mom?"

Alec pulls away, eyes wide and terror running through his veins. He was so sure it was Morgan that he didn't even check on his mom.

He jumps up and pulls out his phone. It rings and rings before voicemail picks up. Alec is pacing with one hand holding the phone to his ear while the other one grips the top of his head.

Morgan slips into a sweatshirt before grabbing Alec's arm. "It was probably just a dream. But let's go check on her." She pulls him out of her room while his phone continues to ring in his ear. As they walk down the hall, Morgan peeks her head in Patrick's open door. "We're going to check on Alec's mom. It's probably nothing."

She slips on her shoes and grabs her purse by the front door before they leave.

EMILY COLLAPSES in the middle of the War room. Mark enters, running to her as she attempts to pick herself up with tears streaming down her face.

Mark kneels next to her, and she looks up to him, unable to hide the fear and misery. She wraps her arms around his neck and cries into his shoulder while he holds her.

After a moment, she pulls herself together but doesn't let go. She uses the physical touch as a conduit. She reaches into his psyche, and before he catches on to what she's doing, she erases his memories from the last few days and implants false ones.

More tears fall when she pulls back, and Mark stares at her with a blank expression. She guides him out of the war room, out of the control room, and up the basement stairs. She releases him in the foyer and wipes her tears, putting on a convincing smile, then releases Mark from his trance.

"That's so exciting! Where are you going again?"

Mark beams at her. "Hawaii. It'll be fun. I just wish you could come with us."

"You will have fun without me. Give Samantha and Dan my love, and enjoy the trip. And buy a fourth ticket for that special lady you've secretly been seeing."

"You know about that?"

"Yeah. I'm glad you're happy."

Mark pulls Emily in, kissing her forehead before he lets go. "I'll see you in a few weeks. Call if you need anything."

"I will, dad."

He directs his eyes toward the stairs. "Bye, Jerrick. Take care of my girl."

Jerrick nods. "I'll do my best."

With that, Mark opens the door. Emily watches him until his taillights disappear.

They don't notice Lathe as he enters the room, too engrossed in Mark leaving. Lathe hangs back, leaning on the pristine white walls, too tired to care if he's getting them dirty.

Emily finally closes the door and turns back toward the foyer. Jerrick steps in front of her. "You sent him away."

The tears begin again as she looks up at him. "Things are bad, Jerrick. Really bad."

"What happened?"

"I saw it. Everything Ashley predicted. I saw it all from Evelyn's mind."

He steps toward her, reaching out to pull her against him. "It's okay. We will deal with whatever comes."

She pulls back, her lips pursed and a crease forming between her brows. With a little headshake, she takes another step backward. "It doesn't make sense. The day Evelyn died, she squeezed my hand and told me I was a strong leader with an amazing team, and that we had a fighting chance with Ashley working as a liaison between the Olvasho and the Latovian people. She said great things would happen. But where are these great things, Jerrick? She saw the same future I did, so what am I missing? How do we stop the inevitable future?"

"Maybe we don't." Lathe's voice echoes from across the marble foyer. He pushes off from the wall and moves toward them.

Turning toward Lathe, Emily gasps, before narrowing her gaze on him.

Jerrick sighs. "Please tell me that isn't Latovian blood all over you."

Lathe motions to his blood-soaked body with a shrug. "This was totally unnecessary by the way. As it turns out, wearing the blood of a Latovian is a myth. I'd be dead if it weren't for my Latovian grandfather. And I only went because Ashley begged me."

"Did anyone see you like that?"

Lathe nods. "Wolfe, Deja, and Ashley before she got sucked into a tornado of wild Latovian blood magic and disappeared—maybe forever." He swallows. "Wolfe is keeping things from us."

"Like what?

"His magic is stronger than I knew, and I think he can summon dragons. Deja was terrified of Wolfe tonight. I've never seen her afraid of him. She told me we shouldn't save Latovia. She said she didn't want to die, but it was too dangerous."

"Where is she now?"

"Downstairs. She was still shaken up. She's not telling me everything."

Emily sighs. "It's gotta be dragons, right?"

Jerrick rubs his temples. "I'm surprised you didn't go after Ashley."

"I did, but my gifts are stunted down there, and Wolfe knows those caves better than anyone. He doesn't want her to die either." His gaze slides to Emily. "I'm here to help you figure out how to break the curse because I don't care what Deja says, I will fight for Latovia until I know Ashley and Deja are safe."

Emily crosses her arms. "That's a sweet sentiment, but

none of us know how to break the curse. I've searched books. I've gone through all my repressed memories. I've even tried looking it up online. Do you have a clue how to break it?"

"I'm pretty sure the Valla born has to go into Latovia to do it."

She rubs her forefingers between her brows. "Oh, great. So, Latovian blood will get me through the door, but I'll die before I can save anyone." Her fingers run through her hair, pausing halfway through. Her head shoots to Jerrick. "Maybe that's it. Maybe, I have to die. Maybe the dragon kills me and takes my ashes back to Latovia to free them all."

His eyes narrow. "Do you believe that?"

"I don't know. It makes sense. Maybe that's why the vision always ends there."

"Even if there are dragons in Latovia. Ashley would never command a dragon to kill you."

"That's what she kept telling me, but I also never thought I'd torture you guys. Just yesterday, I almost killed Jerrick. There is too much we don't understand to make those promises."

"Is there anything else you remember from the vision to help us predict how soon this will happen. Like the weather, or is it a full moon?"

"It was definitely nighttime. It was warm. The trees had all their leaves, and the grass was dry enough to burn without causing an immediate wildfire. I don't remember seeing the moon, but the sky was really smoky."

Lathe shrugs. "That gives us something."

"When did it rain last?" Emily asks.

Jerrick sighs. "Last week."

⤜⤏

ALEC RUNS INTO HIS HOUSE, knocking on his mom's bedroom door before entering.

"Mom!" He rushes into her room and watches her stir. "Mom?"

She sits up in bed, reaching for the light on the night-stand. "Alec, sweetie, what's wrong?"

He slumps on the bed next to her, wrapping her in a hug. "You didn't answer your phone."

She blinks, spotting Morgan in the doorframe. "Were you calling me? Where were you? I thought you were in your room."

"I was, but I had a bad dream. I went to Morgan's to check on her but thought maybe something had happened to you."

Cindy gives a reassuring grin. "I'm fine, just worried about you and I might go crazy if I have to keep pretending I don't know the two of you are a couple."

Morgan steps into the room. "And what about you?"

Cindy blanches, sitting up straighter while Alec looks at her wearily. "Mom?"

Morgan blushes. "We ran into each other the other night. He was sneaking in while I was sneaking out."

"What?" Alec laughs. "Mom, are you getting some on the down-low?"

"I thought you'd be upset."

"Fuck, it's not dad, is it?"

She pulls back. "Good God, No!"

Alec smiles. "I'm happy if you're happy. Who is it? Do I know him?"

Cindy's eyes slide to Morgan, who grins with an encouraging nod.

"It's Mark."

Alec squints, before saying, "Mr. Burk? Emily's dad?"

Their roles reversed, Cindy gives a tentative nod as she fiddles with her blanket while she waits for his reaction.

"He seems like a good dude."

Cindy smiles. "He is a good dude."

Morgan tugs at Alec's arm. "Come on. We've interrogated her enough. Let her go back to sleep."

Alec kisses his mom's cheek. "I'm happy for you."

As soon as he steps out of her room, his smile falters. That feeling of something being very wrong returns, and he can't seem to shake it. They go to Alec's bedroom, where Morgan talks him into bed, trying to reinforce that it was just a bad dream.

CONNECTION

18

Alec reaches across the bed, searching for Morgan, but finds her spot empty. The morning sun is peeking through the window blinds. He sits up, grabbing his phone from the nightstand, but accidentally picks up Morgan's instead. After seeing it's eight am, he rolls out of bed. Wearing nothing but the shorts he slept in, he goes in search of Morgan.

He hears talking from down the hall and follows the noise. He's running a hand through his hair as he enters the kitchen.

He finds Morgan sitting at the kitchen island, sipping her coffee. She gives him a tentative grin. "Good morning."

He smiles, stepping toward her before noticing the others. His mom stands with her back to the oven, and her arms around Mark, the boyfriend he just learned about. Alec drops his arm and his smile simultaneously. Hearing about them was one thing, but seeing them together fills him with a fit of protective jealousy. He trusts her, but he's always been his mom's number one guy. He knows that's bound to change, and he doesn't like it.

"What's going on?" he asks.

Cindy pulls away from Mark and beams at her son. "Mark is taking me to Hawaii!"

A million things run through Alec's head, and he turns to Morgan, who wears the same concerned expression.

"Mark, I thought you were staying with Emily."

"I just got back from my visit. It was her idea for me to invite your mom. Sam and Dan are coming too."

Morgan excuses herself, walking toward Alec's room while he questions, "Sounds like a family vacation. Is Emily going?"

"No. She couldn't get away."

Cindy slips away from Mark and steps toward her son. "Baby, I don't have to go. I know this is all new to you."

Alec shakes his head. "You should go. When do you leave?"

"Tomorrow," Mark answers.

Alec nods, and Cindy comes toward him. "Alec, honey, you sure you're okay with this?"

"Yeah, mom. You're an adult. You can do whatever you want, and I'm happy for you." He reaches out, gripping her shoulders. "You deserve this trip," he says before pulling her close and squeezing her tight.

After a moment, he steps back. "I'll give you two some alone time." Without waiting for a response, he leaves the kitchen and goes straight to his room, where Morgan is on the phone.

She pulls her mouth away from the phone, saying, "I'm talking to Jerrick."

∽◦◦

PATRICK SITS UP IN BED, feeling her at the confines of his mind. Instead of fighting to break their connection, he faces her so he can tell her how much he doesn't appreciate her invading his mind.

He lies back and closes his eyes, finding her in the middle of a burning field. Deformed dragons fly overhead as fire rains from the sky. She's trying to run, but she's moving too slowly, like she's walking with cement blocks strapped to her feet.

He wonders how she reached out to him while she was mid-nightmare.

He moves to her side, observing her slow-motion run before calling her name.

She spins to him in regular speed, her eyes widening. She clings to him, her arms around his middle, her head buried against his chest.

After a moment, she pulls back, her tear-filled eyes looking up at him. "You came back."

Her desperation softens his response. "Emily, you're dreaming. The dragons haven't come. Everyone is okay."

Her hands grip his shirt, and she pulls him out of the way as a dragon swoops down, blowing fire. She redirects the wind, shifting the flames while Patrick falls forward, landing on a knee. She stands between him and another approaching dragon—this one larger. She shoots flames out of her hands, and the dragon screams and retreats. But they keep coming.

Wrapping herself in her own flames, she moves toward the approaching hoard.

Patrick watches in fascination as she wipes them out one

after the other. When she turns back to him, she's wearing a triumphant smile. She moves toward him, and her flames recede, her bare skin peeking through where the fire burned through her clothes. He keeps his eyes on her face, noticing she doesn't look the least bit embarrassed, nor does she appear to be trying to seduce him. She walks straight to him like nothing has changed.

"You're naked."

She looks down at her body with a shrug. "That keeps happening. Hardly seems important anymore."

"Emily, why do you keep reaching out to me?"

"Is this really the time to have this conversation?" A dragon comes out of the smoke, and Emily turns to face it, her mind creating the distraction.

Patrick steps between her and the dragon, and mentally reshapes the dream, taking them away from the dragon war to a crystal blue lagoon where a waterfall flows from a cliff in the background. They stand on the rocks at the water's edge, feeling a fine misting from the thunderous waterfall.

Emily flinches, her arms lifting to protect herself from an unseen threat. "What the hell?"

"You're safe," he reassures before removing his t-shirt.

Her arms fall, and her eyes turn sad. "Safety is just an illusion."

He holds out his shirt to her. "Put this on."

She pulls the shirt on. "It doesn't matter where I go. I can't outrun my future." She looks up at him. "I'm sorry, Patrick. I know you felt me in your head while you were with that girl. That was unfair of me. You deserve happiness."

"You're right. I do."

Her chest falls, and her eyes close.

He grips her shoulders. "Nothing was going on between that woman and me. The only reason I reacted to her at all was because I could feel you watching."

Her brows draw together as her eyes narrow. "What do you mean?"

"I mean, I stopped it as soon as I felt you leave my mind."

"You did it to make me jealous?"

"I did it because you have no right to barge into my head whenever you—"

Her eyes shift, and she shoves him back into the water. She's right behind him as flames from the sky assault them. She pulls him deeper as fire hits the water above, and the shadow of dragon wings flap away. They hold on to one another under the water. And when the coast is clear, they come up for air. While Emily searches the sky, Patrick watches her, their arms around one another while their bodies touch from hip to chest.

When she brings her focus back to him, their faces align, and her breath falls against his lips as she gasps. His arms run up her back, his t-shirt a delicate barrier.

She looks at his lips, her hands already tucked behind his neck. "Patrick?" Her hands slide up into his hair, her fingernails grazing his scalp. "Please come back to me."

He parts his lips, inching forward until they make contact. The shrill peal of his phone interrupts their moment, and Emily fades from his arms as their connection dissolves. A white ceiling replaces the blue sky surrounding the lagoon, and he rolls over to grab his phone, fighting the urge to chuck it across the room.

He answers with a curt, "What?"

It's Morgan. "Emily is sending her family to Hawaii.

Mark doesn't seem the least bit concerned. They leave tomorrow."

He rubs a hand over his face. "She manipulated him."

"Yeah. I just talked to Jerrick. Emily believes she's meant to die."

LATHE STANDS, looking out the library window. He's avoided the library since the day his mother died. Anytime he looks out this window, with the perfect view of the back patio, he still pictures her sitting out there with Emily on the bright spring day. There was no warning that something terrible was about to happen, not like today. Today, the overcast sky gives off the feeling of doom and gloom.

After seeing how his mother and Ashley and even Emily were affected by seeing the future, he's grateful that skill wasn't passed on to him. A chill runs through him, and he runs a hand over his scalp, feeling the prickle of hair. He hadn't shaved for a couple days. He always kept it trimmed close to the scalp since his scars left his hair patchy.

He was still running his hand back and forth over his head when Emily interrupts him.

"Hey."

His hand pauses, and he pulls up the hood of his hoodie before turning to face Emily. "Did you get any sleep?"

"I did. Thanks for the sleeping pills."

Lathe swallows. "Deja's gone. When I went to check on her last night, she wasn't there. She could be anywhere. She could've gone back to Latovia, or she could be hiding in the walls of the mansion."

She gives him a look of sympathy, and her voice is gentle. "She knew you'd try to interrogate her. She may know exactly what's going on, but they're still her people. It's hard betraying the people who raised you."

"I raised her."

Emily tilts her head with a shrug. "You're her friend. She looks up to you, but Wolfe is her family. The orphans are her family. So as much as she wants to protect you, she's too loyal to betray her people."

"They're my people too. Latovians helped raise me."

"It sounds like Wolfe made it clear. They aren't your people."

The secret door in the bookshelf creaks open and they turn with bated breath. A little girl comes through, but it's not the girl they were hoping for.

This girl's skin isn't as pale, and her hair isn't quite as dark a Deja's.

"Wendy," Lathe greets, "I haven't seen you for a while."

"We've been ordered not to visit you anymore."

"Why?" Lathe asks.

"Because of me?" Emily questions.

The girl shakes her head. "Because every time a portal door opens, the magic in Latovia weakens."

Lathe and Emily exchange a look of concern. "So why did you come now?"

"Deja is to return with me. Our king demands it."

"Why?" Emily takes a step toward her. "What does Wolfe want with her?"

The girl pales. "It's not my place to ask."

Emily's magic sizzles across her skin. "But if you had to guess?"

Wendy's eyes grow wide, and she chews at her lip. "I . . . I don't know."

Lathe intervenes. "You can tell him we don't know Deja's whereabouts. We thought she returned to Latovia."

The girl focuses on him. "Are . . . are you sure you don't know?"

Lathe narrows his gaze. "How angry is the King?"

She wrings her hands, avoiding his eyes.

His voice softens. "It's okay, you can tell us. It won't go further than this room. You have my word."

She looks up at him slowly, her eyes glazed with tears. "It's scary, bluebird."

Lathe kneels, coming to eye level with the girl. "Tell me."

"The king has ordered all the orphans to stay in our quarters, and families are staying in their homes. The gems go out for hours, and then they'll come back on. Several people are unaccounted for, and Deja is one of those. If she isn't with you then maybe . . . maybe she was abducted by the thing that keeps taking everyone."

Lathe shakes his head. "No, Deja is too sneaky for that. How did you get to us?"

"The king got me. He walked me to the portal door. He's waiting there for me." A tear streaks her face. "I can't go back empty-handed."

Lathe wonders if Deja is in the walls, listening to her orphan sister's plea. "What about Ashley? Have you heard anything about the queen?"

She wipes her face. "The queen was taken with the others. She's missing. But we think she may have let herself be taken. She could be trying to save everyone who is missing."

Lathe closes his eyes, turning back toward the window. He pictures it over and over in his mind—the fog creeping towards him on the cave floor—the look on Ashley's face and the moment she decided to sacrifice herself. He hits the wood frame of the window. "Damn it!"

Wendy trembles, and Emily moves in to comfort her, touching her shoulder gently. "It's okay. He's just worried about Latovia. And it's frustrating that we don't know how to help."

Wendy's voice quivers. "Aren't you gonna save us?" She looks up with tears running down her cheeks, and Emily's face falls.

"Yes." Lathe answers, spinning back to them. "Yes, we are. She is. Emily is doing everything in her power to save Latovia. We just don't know how the curse works, but we're figuring it out."

"You mean, you don't know how to save us?"

Emily swallows. "Not yet, but I have a good idea."

Lathe flicks his eyes to her just as she says, "Have you seen any sign of dragons?"

Wendy gasps. "Are dragons real? I've heard about dragons, but they died before I was born, if they ever existed at all. I thought it was just a tale the adults liked to tell to make them feel better about being trapped."

"We'd better get you back to Wolfe." Lathe says.

"You're right." She turns back toward the bookshelf, but Lathe stops her by placing a hand on her shoulder.

He says, "You don't have to go back that way. We'll take the easier route."

They escort her down to the portal door. As they ride the elevator to the tunnel below the mansion, Lathe says, "Earlier you mentioned the portal doors, plural. How many are there?"

"This is the portal we use the most because of you, but there are hundreds of them. They take us all over the world, but most are forbidden because once you leave, you can't come back. It's one way only. This portal looks like a door, but even the portals that go both ways rarely look like doors from the outside. There are only twenty with strong enough magic that we know we'll be able to return. We don't even know where some of them lead. If someone doesn't come back, we assume that door is one way."

"Where do the twenty lead?"

"All over. A place called Indonesia, Florida, Madrid, New York, Russia. This is the safest one because it's hidden. And because of you."

Emily gives her a warm smile. "Tell Wolfe, we'll keep an eye out for Deja. Be safe, Wendy."

Wendy nods, her hand turning on the portal doorknob.

Once she's gone, Lathe and Emily watch the carved wooden door shift back to black steel.

Emily says, "Wolfe thinks we won't save Latovia if it means releasing dragons on the world." She looks at Lathe. "Wouldn't you lie?"

EMILY LEANS OVER HER DESK, the words on the page blurring as her tired eyes fight to adjust.

Suddenly, the book closes with a thud and Emily jerks back, realizing it's only Jerrick. He shut her book. "Emily, you need sleep."

"But we aren't any closer."

"And you won't accomplish anything in the shape you're in. Get some sleep. We can start fresh in the morning."

She looks to Lathe, needing his permission to quit for the night.

He nods and Emily yawns.

When Emily crawls in bed, she's sure her anxiety will keep her awake, but she's so exhausted that she falls asleep almost immediately.

Her dreams are bizarre and stress-driven.

She's in the underground tunnel and everything is on fire. Bricks are falling from overhead. She's dodging them when Patrick finds his way into her dream. She isn't sure whether she sought him out or if he found her, but he's there with her in the stress dream that she wishes she could wake from. He's too real for him to be just a part of the dream, and his thoughts don't align with hers, which seems to give him some control over the dream.

"What are you doing here?" she shouts over the noise of crashing bricks.

"You brought me here!" he says, wearing only his boxers. He dodges a brick. "Why is the ceiling caving in? Make it stop."

"I can't."

In a flash, he's standing in front of her with his hands on her shoulders. "Yes, you can because this is all in your head. Just picture what you want."

Picturing what she wants is dangerous because as soon as she imagines it, they are standing in her bedroom with rose petals everywhere. "Umm."

The briefest expression of sadness crosses his face before

he covers it with a blank-unreadable stare. She expected a smirk if anything, but she keeps forgetting this is the same Patrick that left her. His rejection stings, making her twitchy. "I umm didn't mean to bring us here."

"At least bricks aren't falling on us," he says, moving to the door.

She follows him out into the hall, relieved the flower petals stopped at the door. "I didn't mean to draw you into my dream. I didn't do it consciously."

His hand pinches the back of his neck and he turns to face her, his eyes hard. "Are you bringing me here to say goodbye?"

She lets out a breath. "What?"

"You're sending your family to Hawaii."

"Yeah."

"Because you think you're gonna die."

She stares at him, trying to understand his anger, but his stare is unwavering.

"I didn't bring you here to say goodbye. I didn't mean to bring you here at all."

"In that case, I'll be on my way." He disappears before she can say another word.

She expected more of a reaction, especially after last night. She had begged him to come back, and he had kissed her before abandoning that dream too.

LOVE

19

EMILY IS IN HER ROOM, searching through old journals from Olvasho who died a hundred years ago. They'd found them early this morning, hidden in the basement of this estate. She jumps as her phone rings.

She searches for the phone hidden among the books. Pulling it out, she answers.

Through the phone, Morgan says, "You're not giving up, are you?"

Emily sighs. "It's not like I want to, but I've seen what's going to happen."

"Then prevent it."

"I've tried." She paces the floor of her bedroom, her feet walking the wood floor as if each plank is a balance beam. "It's hard not to feel hopeless right now. I have more questions than answers, and the only thing I know for sure is that we're running out of time. Our alliance with the Latovian people has always been a fragile thing built on trust. That trust has been violated but backing out of our union means damning all of Latovia, and we can't let Ashley and all those kids die."

With a gentle voice, Morgan says, "I heard Ashley and Deja are missing."

Emily sighs. "Ashley was swept up by the same wild magic that is overtaking Latovia. There are dozens of people missing. Most of them orphans. And Deja warned Lathe not to break the curse—not to trust Latovians. But she was vague, and now she's missing too. I'm trying to prevent a catastrophe and have no idea how, but if these visions are accurate, then Ashley is okay and has picked Latovia's side. If my death solves everything, then maybe I need to die by dragon fire."

Morgan says, "I thought your skin doesn't burn."

"My magic flames don't burn me. It doesn't mean I'm immune to fire."

Emily waits for a response, her feet stopping in front of her bedroom window. She stares out over the back of the estate. The sprawling meadow in the center is bordered on all sides. Stables line one side of the property, with a lake on the other while a forest of trees covers the back of the lot.

At the front of the estate, towering hedges line the property, hiding it from prying eyes. The closest neighbors are a quarter-mile away on either side, but the Olvasho had bought out those properties years ago. The exteriors of the homes have been preserved, but it is all an illusion while their insides sit abandoned and in disrepair.

"Alec and I are coming," Morgan says, breaking her train of thought.

"Don't come here, Morgan. You and Alec should both go with my dad and the others."

Morgan laughs. "In what world do you see that happening?"

"I'm not being cutesy and heroic," Emily says, "I'm being realistic, and if you come here, there is a very good chance you both could die."

Morgan hesitates before asking, "Why are you even giving me an option? You manipulated your dad into leaving. Will you do the same to us?"

Emily turns away from the windows. "My dad would throw himself in front of a bullet if it meant saving me. You aren't as protective of me."

"Emily, I don't think Patrick is coming with us. He's usually open with me, but he's been quiet and moody the last two days." She pauses. "Do you want us to bring Maggie back to you?"

Emily already suspected Patrick wasn't coming, but it hurts to hear it and to know it's her fault. And of course, she wants her dog, but she can't take her away from him. She can't take anymore from either of them. It would be too selfish.

"I didn't expect him to come," she finally says. "And he should keep Maggie."

EMILY SENSES THE NEW ARRIVALS. She feels Morgan's presence, and she was warned about Alec's flickering aura. She even senses Maggie, but it's the fourth one she's focused on. Patrick came. He's here.

She paces outside her room, feeling unprepared. She runs a hand through her hair and peeks in the mirror, then stops herself, wondering what she's doing. He's not here for her. She shakes that thought away and leaves her room to meet everyone in the foyer.

Jerrick and Lathe are greeting the new arrivals. Maggie is the first to notice her, and the dog runs, tail nub wagging toward Emily on the stairs. She bends down to pet her, and it seems to draw everyone's attention to her. When she stands up and resumes walking down the stairs, she does her best to avoid looking directly at Patrick.

Too eager and she might scare him away, but too cold, and he's less likely to forgive her. She sneaks a peek at him, but he isn't looking. Instead, he's talking to Jerrick.

Morgan and Alec greet Emily with hugs while Lathe stands fiddling with the strings of his hoodie, pulling the hood tighter around his hollow face. Shadows darken his eyes, proof of sleepless nights and too much loss.

After saying hello to Emily, Morgan leans toward Lathe, touching his shoulder. "How are you doing?"

Lathe jerks away from her touch and steps away as if she'll try again. Scowling at her, he snaps, "My mom just died and a magic that's killing people whisked away the only other person I love. How'd you be?"

Morgan pulls her hand back, her cheeks turning pink. "Sorry."

Lathe walks away and Jerrick pulls everyone's attention to him by gesturing toward the back of the house. "I ordered lunch for everyone. It's in the dining room."

Jerrick and Patrick take the lead, and Alec pulls Morgan into his side. "You okay?"

She nods, and Alec turns to Emily. "How long have you known our parents are dating?"

She shrugs, looking ahead at Patrick. This was going to be a long lunch.

SEATED around the dining table with full plates, the tension in the room is suffocating. It drives Emily crazy the way her nerve endings stand on high alert whenever he's around.

Full plate in hand, Lathe scoots back from the table and stands. "If Ashley were here, she'd call out how fucking awkward this is. I'll be in the basement."

They watch him go, and when Emily looks back to the table, she notices Patrick watching her. Her heart races.

He opens his mouth to ask, "Do you have your head sorted?"

The question comes at her like a punch to the gut. She recoils, catches her breath, and answers with a neutral, "I do."

"Jerrick has been keeping us appraised of the situation, but I'd like to hear your take on what's going on. Is there anything you've been hiding from the rest of the class?"

Jerrick clears his throat, glaring at Patrick. "You will show her respect while you are in this house."

"It's okay, Jerrick," Emily calms him before turning to Patrick with a bored glare. She takes a bite of mac and cheese, chewing, swallowing, trying to rein in her mixed feelings, trying to be rational, but it's impossible to be reasonable around him. Giving up, she sets her fork down and slides her seat back, deciding it's better to leave than to say something she'll regret. He has every right to be angry, but she can't do this in front of everyone.

"Enjoy your lunch," she offers before leaving the room.

"You can't leave," Patrick complains, but she doesn't hear any more of his complaints as she rushes into the foyer and up the stairs.

A minute later, Patrick enters her room without knocking—without any right to do so. He walks to her with an intensity she doesn't understand. Once he reaches her, he stops, just a breath away, stealing her next inhale. She stares at him, breathless.

His face is hard, his iron jaw tight, and his sapphire eyes darker than usual. "You sure you have your head sorted?"

She nods.

His hand touches her chin, lifting it as he looks down at her, his breath tickling her face. "Do you love me?"

She blinks, her eyes filling with tears as she nods. "Yes."

The hand at her chin glides up her jaw, and his other hand joins, cupping her cheeks. "Good," he whispers before he closes the space between them. His lips descend on hers, and her arms go around him, her hands gripping onto him as if she's afraid he'll let go—worried, he'll pull away like it was all a joke. But she feels his own desperation in the way he kisses her—the way he holds her face, so firm, yet so gentle.

He was the forbidden fruit for so long, and now he's here with her after everything they had been through.

He pulls back. "Do you want this, Emily?"

She wonders what kind of question that is, but he isn't finished. "Do you want me?"

She closes her eyes. "More than anything."

His forehead rest against hers as his tension in his shoulders melts away. He turns his face into her neck and begins kissing her there while he peels her out of her clothes. First, her shirt goes over her head and he tosses it across the room.

"Do you want me to stop?"

"No." His touch makes her light-headed.

Next, he pushes her pants down, along with her panties.

He's never been so bold with her, and she's not the least bit interested in stopping him as his fingers roam her bare skin. He unhooks her bra and she pulls her arms out.

His hands run down her body before he begins removing his own clothes. She helps. And when they are standing there in nothing but what God gave them, she grabs ahold of him. His fingers go between her legs, and she gasps, her hands gripping him tighter.

Her cheeks warm. "This isn't how most people do this."

"Nothing we do is normal. Most people kiss before being wrapped naked in bed together, but we've been there a few times."

Her breathing is sporadic, getting heavy with what his fingers are doing to her. She can't think straight, and her legs feel weak. Her breath falls in gasps against his chest. "Patrick," it's breathy as her body undulates.

He pulls his hand away and grips her hips, moving them backward until her back presses against the glass pane of the window overlooking the lake.

Considering how much she's been naked lately after burning through almost all of her clothes, the idea that anyone in the mansion might see them doesn't bother her, though she knows it probably should.

"Emily—"

"Do it, Patrick."

He doesn't ask if she's sure or second guess her choice.

He lifts her up. Her arms drape around his neck, and her legs encircle his hips. He positions himself before entering her all at once.

She gasps, and he lets out a breath. He stills as her face falls against his shoulder.

"Shouldn't we have a condom?" she asks belatedly.

"No."

She's pretty sure that's the wrong answer, but as he begins moving, she forgets to care, getting lost in the sensation. She feels a lot of pressure at first, but it isn't painful like she'd expected. Quite the opposite. She wants more.

"More," she moans, and he loses his gentleness and thrusts forward, holding her body tight against his, but they don't kiss.

The cool glass against her back warms, and she likes the roughness and rawness while being thrust against the smooth glass surface. Push too hard and it could shatter, but she enjoys the risk, the danger, the way he takes charge without feeling like a threat.

"More," she moans.

He doesn't question if he's going to hurt her, or pretend he knows what's best. Instead, he gives them both what they want, trusting so hard, the glass vibrates, as her ass bounces against it. He doesn't take it easy on her. He never has.

And she loves him for it.

Her breast rub against his chest as he grows even larger inside of her. And then he stills, gripping her tight, like he wants their bodies to become one. She feels his release, and as soon as the pleasure dies down, her mind begins conjuring images of little blond babies. She pushes him away, her feet returning to the floor. "Are you trying to get me pregnant? You didn't even try to pull out."

She feels the warm trickle run down her inner thigh.

Patrick smirks, his blue eyes shining with mirth.

She shoves his chest, pushing him back a step. "What's wrong with you?"

She hates how sexy and confident he looks while standing naked in the middle of her room while she's scolding him.

She's about to lose her mind when he steps forward, saying, "I'm sterile."

Her eyes flick to his penis and back to his face.

He laughs. "It still works, but my swimmers can't get to you."

She purses her lips. "But, Sky's plan?"

He shakes his head. "He didn't know. I had the procedure done in secret when I was eighteen. I knew my life was not conducive to child-rearing, and kids would be used as leverage. I didn't want that. Children were a weakness I couldn't afford. I didn't want to care about anyone the way my mom cared about me."

"But Sky?"

"Didn't know."

She sits on the side of the bed. "That means we'll never have children?"

He runs a hand through his hair. "There are options, but that's a long way off, and if I'm being honest, I don't know that I will ever want kids."

"I don't know if I want them either, but I feel like there should be little Patrick's running around someday."

He sits next to her, pulling her closer and kissing her head. "Let's just focus on this right now."

"About that . . ."

Patrick squeezes her. "I'm not letting you sacrifice yourself, Emily. You are not saying goodbye to me. You said you had your head sorted, and you admitted you love me, so you're mine now, and I'll protect you even if it's from yourself."

She leans into him as a tear rolls down her cheek. "You're such an asshole."

Patrick grins and shoves her shoulders. She falls back, laying on her back, and he lowers himself until his face is just above hers. He takes in the tear shimmering in her emerald eyes, and he lowers his mouth to hers, his lips giving her a gentle and reassuring caress. His tongue adds sweetness to the intimate kiss. Until now, they have only ever acted on their desires when the pull was too strong. They stole frantic moments, but this caress is relaxed, unrushed. It speaks of many more moments just like it. It speaks of a future together, and she desires that future more and more with every breath.

"IT'S BEEN A WHILE. Should we go check on them?" Alec asks, still seated at the dining table with Morgan and Jerrick.

Morgan sighs. "They'll either figure it out or kill each other."

Jerrick nods. "In fact, I think they have reached an understanding."

Alec narrows his gaze on Jerrick, "What was that smirk? Can you hear them?"

"No, but Olvasho pick up on thoughts and emotions."

Morgan smiles. "They love each other."

Jerrick changes the subject. "Alec, how are you feeling? You said you felt someone is trying to communicate with you?"

"Yeah. I . . . I think it might be Ashley."

Jerrick leans forward, his elbows landing on the table. "Explain."

"We were talking on the way here and the woman screaming, the indistinct whispers, the way my aura has been spotty, like a Latovian. Ashley healed me in Latovia. In the process, she saw and experienced everything I did, and now, I think I'm experiencing part of her subconscious."

Jerrick raises a brow. "That might explain it. What did Patrick think?"

"He said he and Emily have a similar connection, but he didn't know it was possible to create that link with a Latovian. He thought with the portal and the curse, it would hinder the connection."

"Perhaps it has," Jerrick says. "That's why you flicker. It's like a scrambled television waiting for a signal."

Alec leans back in his seat. "If Ashley was taken by the magic that's killing people, isn't it a good thing that I'm still connected to her? Doesn't that mean she's still alive?"

"Theoretically, yes." Jerrick leans back. "Have you been able to communicate to her?"

"Not really, but until we made the connection that it could be Ashley, I've been trying to avoid it altogether."

Morgan says, "I think it could mean something that it got

stronger after she was taken. Do you think she's asking for our help?"

Jerrick says, "I'm not sure we can help her other than to break the curse, and we're working on that. We know how to open the portal to Latovia, but the second Emily enters, she'll most likely be killed instantly by the curse."

"That's not an option," Patrick says, entering the room.

Morgan looks at him, asking, "Where's Emily?"

"She went to talk to Lathe."

"Did the two of you work things out?" Morgan asks with an eyebrow waggle.

Patrick looks at her. "Yeah, I just went up to help her with a problem she was having. You know, like Alec helps you with your problems."

Alec throws his head back with laughter, and Morgan glares at him.

EMILY USES the stairs to climb down to the tunnel below the mansion since the elevator doesn't appear to be responding. She suspects Lathe turned it off to avoid being bothered, but it won't stop her.

She had forgotten how dark and crumbly the stairwell is. A chunk of concrete falls down the last few steps, announcing her arrival.

"Dammit!" Lathe cries, "Don't you guys know when to leave me alone?"

Emily rounds the corner to where Lathe had set up all the couches. "No, we don't, but not because you don't make it difficult enough."

"Go away. I want to be alone." He's on a sofa with a laptop and a stack of Latovian books sitting next to him.

"What you want and what you need are different. You need sleep, and so long as you're sleeping, I promise we will leave you alone."

"I've already been through all of those books. We want to help Ashley and Wolfe and Deja. We are trying to work together to save Latovia, even if they end up killing us."

He sits with his head in his hands. "Don't you want to go be with Patrick?"

"Yes, I do. I want to spend time with the people who matter because soon, I may not have the chance. We are elbow deep in shit, but I'm going to keep on living and breathing until the shit's up to my eyeballs. And even then, I will fight to spend more time with the people I love, and you and Ashley are part of that list."

"That's a gross metaphor."

She sits down next to him. "Well, I hope it's a picture you'll remember. I don't want you to suffer, but I don't want you to give up either. You need to rest and regain your energy so you can keep fighting. If not for yourself and Ashley, do it for me. In every vision, you and I ride into battle side by side. I'm afraid we're in this together, brother."

"It was safer when I had no one."

"You were a miserable prick when you had no one, then Ashley came around and started calling you on your shit."

"It hurts, Emily. It hurts to live without her and it hurts getting my hopes up. What if we can't save her? Doubt and fear tear me apart and having hope is like sprinkling salt into the fresh wound. What if she can't be saved?"

She takes his hand and squeezes. "Even if it's too late to

save her, we're going to try our best and go down fighting because we don't give up, and we don't let fear make our choices. Ashley and your mom would both tell you not to abandon hope. We haven't gone through all this shit to give up now."

He gives her hand a return squeeze.

She drops his hand as she stands from the couch. "I'm starving. I didn't get to eat earlier. You want to come get dessert with me while the kitchen is empty?"

He glances at her. "Yeah. I'll be up in a minute."

She continues to stand there, waiting on him.

"What," he asks.

"I'm not walking up those damn steps. Fix the elevator."

He presses his lips together and shifts his eyes as he stands from the couch with a sigh.

DIAMONDS

20

EMILY GNAWS AT HER LIP, thinking over the conversation she had with Lathe as she enters her bedroom. She studies the floorboards as she walks to the big window overlooking the back of the estate. The sun had gone down an hour ago, and now the crescent moon plays peekaboo as patchy clouds drift by.

Fireflies flicker across the meadow and a family of deer stroll by the lake's edge. She grabs the curtains and sighs because as much as she loves this view, she can't help but picture the grass burning as smoke fills the air and beasts soar through the sky. Jerking the curtains closed, she turns away, gasping when she sees Patrick watching her from the bed—his gaze penetrating.

She had been so caught up in her thoughts that she hadn't thought about him being there. He's sitting bare-chested with his back to the headboard and legs tucked beneath the lush bedding. Maggie lies next to him with her head on his lap, and a Latovian book propped in his hand. He was likely trying to figure out how to break the curse.

"I've been through that book," she says.

He sets the book down on the nightstand as she moves toward him. Her heart warms, and her troublesome thoughts take a back seat. She could get used to this feeling.

Still fully clothed, she slides into bed next to him, cuddling up to him, and he wraps his arms around her. This is what she needs. More than a declaration of love. More than sex. This—being wrapped in his arms.

Just his presence calms her soul and quiets her mind. She doesn't need to hear his I love yous because they are spoken by the way he watches her, and by the way he embraces her.

She doesn't believe in soul mates, but her soul had certainly met its match. Knowing how important he is, makes her desperate to survive. She has too much to live for now.

"What if I scare you away?" she thinks aloud.

Patrick laughs, running a hand through her hair. "You did."

"That's different. I mean, what if I scare you with how much I love you. What if I suffocate you?"

"Emily, I just came back today, and we've already spent hours apart. What makes you think you're going to suffocate me?"

"When something brings you joy, you tend to cling to it with everything you've got, and I feel like I might do that to you."

"Oh, love, you have no idea how much I want you to smother me. We'll smother each other and become that disgusting couple no one can stand to be around."

She holds him tighter. "That goes against everything I stand for, but I want it so bad. Why can't our lives be easy?"

"Easy would be boring, love. If our lives were too easy, we'd take each other for granted, and we would forget how valuable our love really is."

She pulls back to look up at him. She stares at him, memorizing him before giving in and lifting to kiss him.

Sensing the escalation, Maggie jumps off the bed, and Emily crawls into Patrick's lap, straddling him. Their kiss deepens, passionate and slow. She sighs into his mouth, content, yet wanting. Every step with him is exactly perfect, and she craves more, running her nails across his scalp.

He guides her arms up over her head so he can peel her out of her shirt. Her arms relax around his shoulders as his fingers trace down her collarbone, and skim down the dainty chain of her necklace, stopping on the emerald gem. "I didn't know you still wore this."

"I usually don't, but it reminds me of you and how you saved me."

His eyes lift to hers. "We saved each other."

"Do you want me to take it off?"

"No. Leave it."

She leans in to kiss him but pauses. "Patrick?" she says against his lips.

"Yes, love."

"I fell for you in that underground hideout when you laid in bed with me while I was being so cruel and irrational. You held me, and in that moment, I knew I loved you. I just didn't think it mattered because I was sure my life was over."

She continues, "I realized I was in love with you when you showed up in Chicago and faced Adelaide. And again, when you shoved me into a cold shower after I came on to you. I felt how badly you wanted me. I knew my heart was in trouble. But what you did for me. All those things you did for me. I tortured you, and you still handed me to Ben without a fight. I wanted to scream at you. I wanted you to fight for me, but you didn't try to talk me out of being with Ben.

"I fought so hard not to fall in love with you, but all you would've had to do was kiss me, and I would've been yours. But you didn't. You're better than that, and I was so unfair to you."

Patrick lets out a slow breath. "You terrify me, love, but not for the reasons you think. There is nothing in my life that is more important to me than you, but a relationship with me may not be easy. When I'm with you, I'm not thinking about Sky, but that could change. I'm worried I might have a flash-back, and it'll mess things up between us. I'm afraid of a lot of things, but my love for you is stronger than my fear."

Emily presses her hand against his chest. "I know a rela-tionship can't be easy for you after the way Sky treated you. If anything is ever too much or you need a break, I'll give you want you need—anything you need, no matter what it is."

He places his palm on her neck, his thumb caressing her cheek. He dips his face and pulls her in, but his lips stop an inch from hers. "I'm going to kiss you now to make up for all those times I couldn't."

His sapphire gaze is penetrating, and she feels excite-ment boil within as his gaze flicks to her lips and he slowly lowers his mouth to hers. She kisses him back, unable to stop herself from gripping onto him. He parts her lips with his tongue, and she opens for him, kissing him back with every emotion she's held back as he consumes her through a kiss.

His fingers tangle in her hair while her hands grip his back and she moans into his mouth.

Patrick pulls back, his pupils dilating as he looks at her. "You completely undo me, love."

"Patrick," she pants, feeling her body liquify. "I am so in love with you."

He pulls her back in and spends the next hour showing her all the ways he's been dying to love her.

DEFORMED dragons attack from the sky. One lands next to Emily and she freezes as the creature three times her size walks toward her. A gelatinous membrane covers its body, oozing, like the beast had been descaled and skinned. Its pungent smell causes her to gag, and she takes a step back, her foot getting stuck in the mud.

The dragon opens its mouth as it nears her, and fire sparking up its throat, catching fire as it leaves the beast. The flames hiss towards her.

She wakes gasping for air. The room is dark, and when she moves; she feels Patrick's arms tighten around her. She blows out a breath, and her eyes fall closed in relief.

"What's wrong?" Patrick murmurs.

"Nothing. Everything is fine. You can go back to sleep."

She cuddles into him and he quickly dozes off, but she doesn't. Too many things fill her head, questions, worries, fears. Did the Latovian people skin their dragons alive?

She thinks back over her conversation with Lathe, her mind racing. She loves Ashley, but not the way Lathe loves her, and not the same as she loves Patrick. If Patrick never came back, she would feel like she was missing a piece of herself. Every second would be a second without him, every breath, a breath deprived of him. Time would exist in two periods. There would be pre-Patrick and post-Patrick.

She gets out of bed, feeling too much of a responsibility. She needs to save Ashley—save Latovia, for herself, for Lathe, and for all those who would suffer.

She pulls on her robe and leaves her room, going to the library, thinking if Lathe is awake, that's where she will find him.

She enters and finds it empty and dark. She sighs, relieved he's not here, and hoping it's because he's sleeping. She goes to the window that overlooks the lake, and the door creaks open behind her.

"What are you doing in here?" Lathe asks, flipping on the light as he walks in.

Emily stares at her reflection in the darkened window. The emerald gem at her neckline glints in the dim light, and her eyes get stuck on it.

Her fingers come up, caressing the Latovian jewel. She wonders if an Olvasho stole it from Latovia, or maybe it was a gift.

She turns to him. "Lathe, I know if a Latovian leaves Latovia, they die instantly, unless it's the new moon, but what happens when an Olvasho goes to Latovia?"

"They die."

"How?"

"Latovian power kills them."

She narrows her gaze. "Like how the magic tried to kill you?"

"No, Wolfe said it's more immediate. They go catatonic

almost immediately, and then their bodies give out within seconds, or at most, a few minutes. By the time he gets to them, they're already unresponsive or dead. He's been unable to save any of them."

"What did you feel?"

Lathe frowns. "Latovia weakened me. I felt the pull of magic prickle at my skin. It made me dizzy, and I couldn't think with all the indistinct whispers in my head. Ashley had been complaining about them."

"What does Wolfe say about the whispers?"

"Nothing. He's never mentioned them before, and I think Ashley was afraid to ask him. She seemed pretty certain he didn't hear it."

Emily paces, thinking—contemplating, before concluding, "Remember the basketball-sized gem Ashley brought out of Latovia to capture Adelaide? Remember how it called to all of us, whispering promises of power. It was calling us—tempting us. If one rock is that tempting, then imagine what a whole cave full could do.

"I think we die when we enter Latovia because its power consumes us. You're part Latovian, which is why it didn't consume you, but you felt it, it made you feel sick, and you heard its whispers."

He shakes his head. "Magic doesn't talk."

She steps forward. "No, it doesn't, but it has a voice. The voices of all those it has consumed."

"I feel like you're telling me ghost stories," Lathe says with a raised brow.

"Essentially, I am, but this ghost story is real. I have to go to Latovia. If I can endure the temptation, then I can break the curse."

"How?"

"If I can stand up against Latovia's power, then I might be able to break the enchantment. That or it will consume me," she says with a shrug and a smile.

"When are you going?"

Her eyes shift while she deliberates. "Not tonight."

"Because of Patrick?"

"Because I'm not prepared. I need sleep, and I need to test a theory. Do you have any other gems from Latovia?"

Lathe starts to shake his head no, but stops and says, "Come with me."

She follows him down the hall, and he stops at a hall closet. He steps inside the walk-in and holds the door for her. Then he goes to a large chest of drawers, pulling open the top, middle, and bottom drawers. As soon as all three are out, the dresser shifts to the side, and an opening appears in the wall. They walk through into an unfamiliar wing.

"What is this, and why hasn't it been renovated?"

Lathe shakes his head. "This is the original home. The rest of the estates was added later, but this is where my grandmother grew up with her parents. No one is allowed in this wing, which is why it's hidden."

They move down a musty smelling, creaky hallway, and enter a cobweb lined room. Lathe goes straight for the wardrobe. He pulls out a black jewelry box with a glass lid. He sets the large box of diamond jewelry on a table by the door. Opening the case, he says, "I was told these were all grandma's diamonds, but the diamond I gave Ashley turned purple as soon as she put it on. My magic appears iridescent or sometimes clear, so perhaps these are all Latovian stones.

Most of these were gifts from my grandfather, so it makes sense they'd be Latovian."

Emily reaches down, asking, "What'd you give Ashley?"

Lathe sighs. "An engagement ring."

Her mouth falls open. "You're engaged?"

He nods, his eyes avoiding hers.

Emily reaches to touch a diamond bracelet, and the simple touch turns the whole bracelet into emeralds. "Yeah, I'd say they're Latovian."

Her fingers tingle where they connect to the gems. "Can I borrow these?

"Sure. What are you thinking?"

She picks up the box of jewelry. "I'm not sure yet, but I can figure that out tomorrow after I've slept."

Lathe leads the way back to the halls Emily is familiar with, but before they part ways, he asks, "Do you want another sleeping pill?"

"No. If anything, I'll force Patrick to make me sleep."

QUICK TRIP

21

A KNOCK at the bedroom door wakes Patrick. He knows Emily was up most of the night, so he tries not to wake her as he climbs out of bed. He steals her robe and tiptoes across the room and opens the door, stepping out into the hall.

Jerrick looks him over before saying, "Have you heard of a man named Jamison Platt?"

Patrick nods.

Jerrick asks, "He was a follower of Sky, wasn't he?"

"Yes," Patrick says like he isn't wrapped in a too-short women's robe. "He was an exceptionally creepy guy."

"He's suspected of an Olvasho power killing," Jerrick tells him. "Do you know where we might find him?"

Patrick's brows pinch together as he thinks. "Yeah, at least I used to know. Platt had an underground bunker. Very into doomsday prepping. There's no address, but it's not far from here, only twenty minutes or so. I could drive out and pick him up.

"No, we aren't ready to engage. We just need to know where to find him if the claims are valid.

"Sure. I could get the coordinates. I won't get too close."

"That would be helpful. Thank you." Jerrick's face changes, all the professionalism gone. "Emily is family to me, and you know what I do to people who hurt my family."

"Yeah. I heard about Keith."

"I hope I'll never have to do the same to you."

Patrick snickers. "So much for our history."

Jerrick's voice grows softer. "I know your intentions are good, but make sure they stay that way."

"I'll get you the coordinates in about an hour." Patrick closes the door softly and moves back to the bed.

As he crawls in, Emily mumbles, "What was that about?"

"Jerrick was asking for coordinates to a likely Olvasho murderer. I told him I'd get the coordinates. It's close. I'll only be gone for an hour."

She sits up. "What time is it?"

"It's eleven."

She looks at him. "I'll go with you."

"No, you won't. You were up most of the night. You should've woken me up so I could've helped your mind rest."

"You woke eventually."

"Yeah, at six! Go back to sleep, love. I'll stay with you until you fall asleep."

She lies back with a yawn. "I guess if you insist."

Patrick smirks. "Did you find any answers last night?"

"Kinda, I have a theory."

"Care to share?"

"I can't. My boyfriend is forcing me back to sleep."

"Smart man. Don't worry. I'll be back before you wake."

"But Patrick—"

"Emily, the visions show the attack happening in the night. It's only eleven. I promise you; I'll be fine. Don't worry."

"There is always room to worry."

He leans in, kissing her temple and brushing her hair away from her face. "I promise. No heroics. All I'm going to do is drive there and back." He uses his gifts to subdue her, guiding her into sleep.

SITTING on the couch in the underground tunnel, Alec startles when Morgan places her hand on his shoulder.

"Alec, did you hear me?"

He looks at her, his leg bouncing anxiously. "What?"

She begins talking and his eyes shift away, going to the black steel door, the portal that could take him to Latovia. If only he could go through.

"Alec!" Morgan shouts.

His eyes shift to her, confused by her outburst. Indistinct whispers fill his head so he can't hear what she's shouting. He stands and walks toward the portal.

"Yesssss, yesssss," the soft voices hiss.

Even without Latovian blood, the steel door morphs. The carved wooden vines glow warm and inviting. He reaches out, his palm resting on the portal's doorknob.

His hand drops from the knob as he is forcefully pulled away. He looks back to find Morgan tugging on his arm.

While she hauls him toward the elevator, he twists his

neck, gazing longingly at the portal door. The elevator closes around them and lifts him away from his mission. The whispers scream, crying out for him. They need him. He has to stop the elevator, but Morgan blocks the buttons, covering them with her back. He steps toward her, and she shakes her head.

"Yesss," the whispers encourage, "Stop her."

He is bigger than her, so he knows he can remove her and stop this contraption. He goes at her, but the next thing he knows, he's lying on his back, staring straight up at the elevator ceiling. She had somehow knocked him down.

The elevator opens, and she drags him out by his arms until his body goes airborne and the man with the scars is next to him, walking beside his floating body.

Is he dreaming?

The whispers fade, and he hears Morgan's voice. "I'm taking him away from here. Maybe for the day or maybe forever."

Lathe says to her, "Good idea. He's not himself."

Alec tries unsuccessfully to stand, but Lathe's hold on his body is iron tight. "Would you please put me down?"

Lathe and Morgan turn to him.

"Why?" Lathe asks.

"I want to go into Latovia. It's calling me. She needs me. Ashley must need me for some reason."

Morgan groans, and Lathe says, "That's not safe for you or Latovia."

Alec watches Morgan, her expression—her fear so easy to see. "Okay." Alec says with regret, "Morgan, I think I have to get out of here."

"Lathe is going to help us to the car."

Alec nods, understanding they don't trust him. Feeling shitty about it, he does what he does best. "Lathe, that's so kind of you to carry me to the car, but I'm not into guys."

Lathe glares at him, while Morgan says, "Well, it sounds like he's coming back around."

"If you want, I can drop him on his head," Lathe offers, "Knock some sense into him."

"He's had too much head trauma as is," Morgan comments, opening the front door.

Once they are standing at the car, Lathe lets Alec down onto his feet, and Alec hops into the passenger seat.

Lathe offers, "Let me know if you have any more trouble."

"I will," Morgan says before climbing behind the driver's seat and starting the car.

As they drive away, Alec kisses Morgan's cheek. "I'm sorry. The whispers just got so loud."

"It's not your fault," she says with a shrug. "None of us really know what's going on."

"Where are we going?"

"Let's get away for a few hours and see how you're feeling."

IT TOOK LONGER THAN ANTICIPATED, because the bastard, Platt, had created multiple bunkers with interconnected tunnels. But Patrick gave all the coordinates he found to Jerrick and is finally on his way back to the mansion. These rural roads are rarely traveled, and Patrick speeds back toward the estate in a hurry. The sun is still hanging high in the sky and he's guessing Emily is still fast asleep. He'll get back and crawl into bed with her, and she won't even know that he took twice as long as he'd said.

He rounds a curve in the road and slams on his breaks. A massive elk stands in the middle of the road, its legs straddling the double yellow line while staring at Patrick. Behind the elk, deer flood the street. The brakes squeal, and the car fishtails before swerving into the grass.

A tree comes at him too quickly, giving him no time to react. The side of the car smashes into the tree, throwing Patrick into the driver's side door. His head splinters the glass with its impact. The car rocks before coming to a halt.

Patrick blinks, his vision blurry as he touches his temple, feeling the trickle of blood. His thoughts go to Emily as everything goes black.

LESSER EVIL

22

Elbows propped on the desk, Wolfe runs his knuckle back and forth across his lower lip, contemplating his options, trying to come up with a better solution. The only feasible strategy he has remaining could cause as many problems as it may fix, but it's his last defense.

It's his people's last hope.

He rests his head in his hands as he says, "Latovia won't last the night. In the last five hours, over thirty-eight people have been reported missing, taken by the wild magic. It's killing them."

"You know what you must do," Midnight says, as he walks across the office to stand in front of the desk.

Wolfe lifts his face out of his hands, tightening his lips as he stares at his oldest friend. He shakes his head. "I can't do that to them."

"You'll do it because it's the only way to save Latovia."

"It's a gamble. I'd be putting everyone at risk."

"You'll have to trust your Olvasho friends to handle it.

They'll realize they need you, and they will free Latovia so we can help them fight this thing together."

Wolfe shakes his head.

Midnight moves forward. "You said it yourself. Latovia will not survive the night."

The king sighs. "Has there been any sign of Deja?"

"No one has seen her."

Wolfe closes his eye, rubbing at his temples, saying, "What if the magic doesn't go after Emily?"

"You know it will. If we drop it in her backyard, it will sense her power and try to feed off of it, but the fire-born Olvasho will sense it coming. It cannot hide in wide-open spaces, not like it hides down here. Give your people a chance."

"We should warn them," Wolfe offers.

"They've been warned. For years, they've known what's to come. They've seen it."

Wolfe nods, tightening his lips as he stands from his desk. "Let's go create a new portal."

Latovia is dim, its magic unpredictable and unstable. They move to the small cavern Wolfe had evacuated the day before.

Midnight creates the portal door on the ceiling of an empty corridor. As soon as the magic is etched into the stone, Wolfe feels the wild magic approaching.

The army of misshapen creatures come at him like a swarm. Most are airborne, flying with uneven wings, while others crawl on four legs. The magic keeping them alive floats heavily in the air, like a thick haze. And in the lead, is his beautiful blonde queen. She rides the wave of wild magic like it's become part of her, interwoven into the very fabric of who she's become.

The swarm stops behind her as she moves toward Wolfe, a cruel smile curling her red lips while her eyes glow purple. "You're smart to let us go, my king."

Wolfe's upper lip curls in disdain. "You're killing the people you swore to protect."

"Or am I making them a part of something bigger?"

As she takes another step forward, Midnight moves between them, and Ashley backs up, eyeing him cautiously. "My king, tell your warrior friend that if he takes another step, my posse and I are so out of here."

"Just go." Wolfe lifts his hand, and the new giant portal door opens wide.

Ashley blows him a kiss as they all disappear through the exit. As the door closes behind them, Latovia shakes as the magic destabilizes even more.

"The magic is feeding on Ashley's magic." Midnight says. "It's using her magic and growing stronger. Prepare yourself, my king. She's not dead yet, but I fear her death is inevitable."

They drove for an hour before impulsively stopping at a movie theater. They are in the middle of their second movie when Alec jumps up. "We have to go back!"

Morgan looks at him wide-eyed. "What?"

"Now!" he insists, "We have to go back now."

Patrons shush him, and he stares at Morgan until she nods and stands, walking for the exit.

When they reach the car, she asks, "What's happening, Alec?"

"Something has changed. The whispers are . . . the magic is loose."

"What?"

"Just drive!"

"I'm calling Lathe," She says, pulling away from the theater.

HAVING COMPLETED A LATE AFTERNOON WORKOUT, Jerrick makes himself a protein shake. He is in the kitchen when he hears commotion from outside. Maggie barks at the back door, and Jerrick looks out the window, watching as monstrous creatures burst from the lake's surface.

Mentally he reaches out to Patrick, Emily, and Lathe, but only Lathe seems receptive at the moment.

"Lathe," Jerrick says mentally.

"I see them," Lathe responds.

"Where are you?"

"In the stables." There is a pause before he says. "Is this it?"

"Not if we can help it." Jerrick moves through the mansion, trying to find Patrick and Emily. Maggie runs ahead.

"What are we supposed to do?" Lathe asks.

"I'm going up to find Emily and Patrick. We fight this thing together!"

MORGAN AND ALEC are almost back to the mansion. No one had answered their calls which made them more desperate to get back.

The sun dips into the horizon, saying its midwestern goodbye, giving them about ten minutes before dusk turns into night.

"Are the whispers getting louder?" Morgan asks as she drives down the road that leads to the mansion.

"No, but the closer we get, the more I sense Ashley."

Morgan bites her lip. "I don't know whether that's good or bad, Alec."

He shrugs. "Me neither."

"Do you think—" Her words are forgotten as she comes across the scene on the side of the road. She sits up straighter and her heart races as she slows the car. "Is that . . . "

Alec notices the car that had collided with the tree. "That's Patrick's car," he says.

As soon as the car shifts into park, Morgan is out, running toward Patrick's car.

When she approaches the driver's side, she sees blood smeared across the broken, bloodstained window.

Alec comes up behind her. "Is he breathing?'

Morgan swallows, her hand shaking as she reaches for the handle. "I don't know."

LATHE IS IN THE STABLES, unlatching the horse's stalls and guiding them out of the barn in case of a fire. Ashley always saw the stables burning in her vision. He guides them out toward the forest instead of the pasture.

"Have you found Emily?" He speaks to Jerrick through their mental link.

"I'm headed up to her room."

Lathe unlatches another stall, but a noise has him spinning around.

Ashley stands a dozen feet away. Her eyes glow purple, and a haze of magic surrounds her. "Hello, Lathen. Say goodbye to Jerrick."

Through their connection, Jerrick says, "Oh, shit. They're inside the house."

Lathe can sense Jerrick shouting, attempting to warn the others before their connection is severed. A window shatters at the back of the mansion, and Jerrick's limp body is carried off by a dragon.

Lathe looks at Ashley, and she grins. "Let's play a game of hide and seek. I hide Jerrick, and you tell Emily to come find him."

She disappears in a cloud of purple magic.

SMOKE & ASH

23

COMMOTION WAKES EMILY, and Maggie is barking outside her door. She picks up her phone on the nightstand and sees it's already eight. She'd slept all day. How could she let that happen, and where is Patrick? She has no missed calls or texts. She reaches out to him using their mental link and can't sense him at all. She jumps out of bed, opening the door for Maggie before pacing and running her hands through her hair.

There has to be an explanation. She grabs her phone again and notices the missed calls from Morgan. She scrolls past them and dials Patrick, but it goes straight to voicemail.

"What the hell, Patrick. Where are you?"

She goes to the window and looks out toward the lake, and Emily watches as shadows fly through the darkening sky. The sun dips below the trees in the distance, but she knows those aren't birds.

Maggie stands guard, while Emily takes a shaky breath and swallows, pulling herself together. She knew this was coming, but whenever Patrick was with her, she let herself dream.

She gets dressed in her fire-resistant outfit, just in case. When she leaves her room, Maggie follows at her side. Emily finds blood in the hall, and a window is broken. She reaches out, sensing no one in the mansion, but Lathe is in the barn. She ventures downstairs and reaches the back doors where her nightmares become her reality as she opens the double doors.

"Maggie, stay."

Maggie sits with a whimper as Emily steps out onto the patio where Evelyn died. She walks by the tables they used as barriers from the gunman. She steps out onto the grass and looks up.

Ashes fall from the sky, and the grass smokes and burns in patches. Two dragons dive towards her from the air, but they collide, and the smaller one's wing snaps while the other soars away. The smaller creature beats harder, its broken wing bending and fluttering in the wind like a ruined kite. It corkscrews downward, landing hard on its feet. Emily hears a crunch as its front legs shatter, and it falls to the ground.

It is no bigger than a pony, but as she approaches, she examines its skin, getting the distinct feeling that this creature was once human. Like a body left in the sun too long, it is bloated with gasses. Its overextended skin seeps, and through the filmy viscous membrane, she sees a broken human skeleton, too small for the frame of this beast, like the creature swallowed a child's skeleton whole. But she knows that's not the case when its grey eyes turn toward her. The face, though warped, looks all too familiar.

She covers her mouth as she realizes who it is. A sob tears out of her at the realization. "Oh my God, Wendy?"

Emily steps forward, tears blur her vision. She wants to save the child, but there is no life to save. The magically misshapen skeleton inside Wendy's skin had obliterated the child's heart. Magic alone is keeping her animated while her body rots away.

Her mother's journal was wrong when it said they create dragons by feeding them children. It is the magic that transforms them into dragons. It's horrific. Unthinkable.

Emily bends down and sweeps the wisps of hair out of the girl's face. "I'm so sorry they did this to you. I didn't know. I should never have let you go back to Latovia. I'm so sorry."

Wendy's monster makes a move to attack Emily, so with a swift swipe of Olvasho magic, Emily slices the monster's head clean off. It causes enough damage that the magic keeping Wendy "alive" abandons the body.

No wonder Wolfe wanted to keep Latovian dragons a secret. No way would Emily save Latovia after seeing what they do to their own flesh. She kneels down to set Wendy's body on fire, but anger surges through her, and she sets the surrounding yard on fire too, the flames shooting up into the night sky.

The dragons swarm and using her flames, Emily shoots them down one at a time, until no more come forward. She continues walking toward the barn with unrelenting angry tears flooding her face.

She pauses when she spots the glowing eyes staring out at her from the cluster of trees beside the pasture. She swallows. Then, as one, the deer step out from the shadows and move toward her, surrounding her.

Absently she reaches out, and a deer nudges its nose against her hand, reassuring her that this is real. Then the elk arrive, moving through the hoard of deer, their antlers looking like barren trees standing tall against the night sky.

Clarity falls over her as she touches the elk from Evelyn's visions. This is always the way it was meant to be. She wonders if Evelyn knew this is how it was supposed to end. She hopes her death means that the others will live. That's the only reason Evelyn would be okay with this, right? There has to be a point, a bigger picture that she can't see.

She looks back at the mansion, wishing she could kiss Patrick one last time. Wishing she could say goodbye to her dad, but this is it—her destiny.

She tried her best to fight it, but as she walks on unsure legs out into the scene straight out of her nightmare, she begins to find peace in the chaos. Her steps steady, and her shoulders roll back. She holds her chin high as she moves through the eerie stillness. Ashes float around her from a battle that's only just begun, but her strides are confident, a side effect of knowing exactly what is about to happen.

She approaches the massive elk from her vision and leaps onto its back, riding to the barn where she finds Lathe sitting on the back of his snow-white horse, his face pale.

Her tangled blond hair blows in the wind, and angry tears continue to carve their way down her soot-covered face. "Those Latovian bastards are turning their children into monsters. These dragons are all made out of people." She points back to where the child's body still burns. "That was Wendy, Lathe."

His eyes shift from her to the fire, and his jaw hardens. His hands grip the reins tighter, and he shakes his head. "Can we save them?"

"They're already dead. Her heart was obliterated by the magic that turned her into that creature."

"I can't believe they'd do this." He itches the scar on the side of his face, one of his nervous habits. "I saw Ashley. She was just here. She took Jerrick to create a trap for you."

"How do you know?"

"She told me."

"Did she look like one of them?"

"No. She looked like herself, but she was dripping with ugly magic."

"Did she have a heartbeat?"

He shakes his head. "I don't know. She seemed to be alive and thriving."

Emily looks over the meadow. "I have to go after Jerrick. There's no other choice."

Lathe says, "I'm going with you."

She looks at him. "You and I both know how this ends, Lathe."

"But it doesn't have to end that way. We do this together!" His horse steps forward. "She went that way." He points across the pasture to the other side of the lake.

They start forward, Emily on her elk and Lathe riding his mare. And all around them are deer.

Lathe struggles to steer through them. "Why deer?"

"I think it's my spirit animal." She moves toward the woods, leading the deer away from the fight and opening a path for Lathe as another wave of dragons make themselves known.

The mansion catches fire, then the stables. Frightened horses run wild across the vast landscape, while Lathe rides on the back of a snow-white horse. As dragons fill the sky, Lathe shouts at the night, his face contorting with anger as he lashes out with violent winds.

Emily's blond hair flows out behind her, her beautiful face dusted with soot and streaked with tears as she comes from the woods riding on the back of a giant horned elk. Following her is a horde of deer leaping out of the woods. She joins up with Lathe in the meadow just as a hippo sized dragon swoops down from the sky, breathing fire.

Emily grabs the horns of her massive elk and rises to her feet on its back. She thrusts an arm out, shooting white-hot flames from her palm. There is no chance for the dragon to dodge the blaze, and as it strikes the beast, its blood-curdling screams penetrate the air, sounding almost human. The creature spirals to the earth, breaking the ground and silencing its cries forever.

Hearing the call of their fallen brother, the dragons swarm, circling the meadow. Their sizes vary, from two-hundred pounds to two-thousand with bat-like wings that span from ten feet to twenty. Dozens of the hideous creatures come from all directions.

Lathe uses the air around him as a weapon, using sharp winds to throw his enemy off course, while Emily uses her gifts to leap onto the back of a deformed dragon flying too close. Her fingers grip onto the slimy skin of the beast, and before it throws her, she melds her mind with it, taking ownership of the magic that is animating the creature.

Its stench is overwhelming, like a rotting corpse mixed with spoiled milk and mold. She forces the dragon up, flying higher into the sky. Her body slips down the creature as a chunk of the dragon's flesh sloughs off in her hand. She cringes, gagging as she drops the fleshy piece and grabs another area of the beast.

Once she's up high enough, she looks around, searching beyond the burned mansion and plumes of smoke covering the ground. Over the next hill, Emily spots what she's looking for and sends the dragon into a dive.

The mother dragon sits on the hillside looking regal. Its forty-foot wingspan dwarfs the others, and her flesh is covered in glistening purple and green scales making her body shimmer. The scales make the dragons flame-retardant, but none of the other dragons have them.

Emily dives through the sky, silent except for her heartbeat hammering. She realizes her dragon's stench is giving her away as the scaled beast sniffs the air and turns to face her. She swerves to the side, and her dragon loses its balance and spirals. Emily lets go and pads her fall, using the air to cushion her landing, while the deformed beast that was once human dies upon impact. These creatures weren't built to last. They were created to kill. Emily rolls up to her feet, and the ground rumbles as the mother dragon stalks towards her.

As it comes closer, Emily doesn't see Ashley on its back. She looks around, wondering where she is. She was there in the vision, so where is she now? The dragon's head tilts to the side, as its purple rimmed eyes glare at Emily.

Emily shouts, "Where is Ashley?"

The dragon lets out a hot breath, lowering its head while its lips curl into a devious grin.

"Not what you expected, is it?" Ashley's voice fills the

air, a deep echoing malice beneath her usual tone. "It's not what I envisioned either, but here we are."

Emily's mouth drops open, and she takes a step back. Ashley *is* the dragon.

"You were smart to let Latovia die. They would've tried to stop this, but you've trapped them in their tomb, and I can't risk you having a change of heart." The dragon takes a step toward Emily.

"Where's Jerrick?" Emily shouts.

"I was going to use him as bait, but decided to make him one of my own instead."

Emily pales, realizing Ashley means to turn Jerrick into one of these deformed fire breathing monsters.

"Ashley, this isn't you."

"You don't know me!"

"What about Lathe? He's over there being attacked by your horde of disfigured dragons."

Ashley's gaze flicks down for a moment before returning to Emily, her voice vibrating with rage, "If those underdeveloped carcasses can beat him, then he deserves to die."

"Just like I deserve to die?"

"I never said you deserve it. It just has to be done."

Without further ado, a thunderous rumbling begins inside the beast that is Ashley. Her neck stretches up, and her mouth opens, filling the heavens with the fires of hell. Then Ashley turns her flames to engulf Emily.

The ground below Emily cracks and she falls into a hole just as the flames reach her.

She hears Ashley's triumphant cry as she falls deeper.

Emily tries to collect the air around her to stop her descent, but monstrous talons wrap around her.

A LOUD CRASH WAKES DEJA. She jumps to her feet, forgetting about the low hanging ceiling. She grabs her head, rubbing the spot where it made contact. She'd been camped out in the attic above the stables for days. She couldn't face Wolfe, not after she betrayed him. She also couldn't face Lathe; afraid she would spill the rest of Latovia's secrets. So, she's been here, hiding away like a coward, and stealing food from the kitchen below.

She looks out the tiny window in the attic, more of a vent than an actual window, but she can see the disaster that lays beyond. Fire rains down from the heavens as the winged demons fly through the night sky, exhaling flames, catching the stables on fire.

She hurries down, slipping between the crack in the wall and sliding down between two pieces of drywall. Even Lathe didn't know about this place, not that he could fit up here, anyway.

Once her feet hit the floor, she shimmies to the side and ends in the utility closet. She slips between the water heater and furnace and opens the closet door, exiting into the kitchen above the stables. She throws open the door and runs down the stairs into the stables.

Instead of getting to Lathe, she runs back into the barn and begins opening the stalls of the horses that remained inside. She tries to shoo the horses out, but they don't listen to her.

The horses run wild circles, freaked out by the flames and by the monstrous noises coming from the creatures breathing fire.

Maggie comes out of nowhere and begins herding the horses, leading them out the back of the barn to areas that aren't yet burning. Once Deja sees they're safe, she runs the other way, toward Lathe and the burning pasture. Deer run aimlessly in the grassy area between the barn and the mansion.

She spots Lathe by the lake on the opposite side of the meadow and decides to run straight through the chaos, dodging hooves and flames. A fiery beast plunges toward her from the sky. She dives under a nearby deer that looks stunned by the fire, and the flying monster strikes the deer, throwing both off course in a horrible tangle of sound.

Deja rolls to a stand, dirt, grass, and soot staining her clothes as she races away from the near miss. She doesn't look back, but the commotion caught Lathe's attention. He's dismounting his horse and sending it toward her at full gallop. The white horse is covered in ash and soot, but still easily spotted from across the darkness.

Flames come from the sky, burning a line straight through the field, cutting Deja off from Lathe. The fearless horse rears back before hitting the wall of fire.

Deja stops, realizing she needs a plan. She can't run blindly. These creatures will kill her.

Not knowing if she'll make it, she shouts, "They're not dragons!"

Lathe is cornered, his back to the water as the monsters come one after the other. He was holding his own until she showed up, but he had to know. She had to tell him these were not Latovian dragons.

Lathe keeps trying to look at her, but she knows he can't

hear her. She screams again, "Those aren't Latovia's dragons."

She has to make him understand this is not her people attacking them.

A shriek from the sky has her spinning toward the giant barreling toward her with its flames blasting. There is nowhere to hide this time. She stands, watching it come for her. Surely, Lathe will understand the Latovians would not attack their own.

Deja stares at the hideous flying monster barreling toward her. She feels the heat from the flames and presses her lip tight to keep from crying. Her nostrils flare as her breath fights to match her rapid heartbeat. She lifts her face toward the flames, determined to stare death in the face, fearless like a true Latovian. Her eyes close as she opens her mouth to let out her final breath.

The next second everything goes quiet and dark. Deja keeps her eyes closed as her breath slows, marveling at how painless death is. Her lids lift slowly, realizing this is not her death. This is magic. A dome of water sits above her head, covering her like a giant upturned fishbowl. Through the transparent blue bubble, she witnesses the raging battle as heavy rain floods the field.

She looks around for the source of magic and finds Patrick standing at the edge of the lake. She notices two others who she assumes are Morgan and Alec. They're rounding the lake, running the same direction Emily had headed. Patrick and Lathe block or kill the creatures who try to attack them. And as the battle leads away from Deja, Patrick releases her from the water cocoon so he can focus all his power toward the other side of the lake where a giant purple scaled dragon sits on the hillside shooting fire up into the night.

Hysterical shouting from the lake and a large water funnel tell her something terrible just happened.

EMILY FALLS. She tries to collect the air around her to stop her descent, but monstrous talons hold her tight. Before she has the time to think about escaping, the talons release her a foot from the ground. She rolls up to her feet from the cement floor and realizes she's in the tunnel under the mansion. The solid black portal door stands just in front of her and she turns to meet the thing that brought her here.

She takes an involuntary step back as she faces yet another dragon, but this one is different.

It towers above her, covered in varying sizes of royal blue and navy scales. It has four muscular legs with long talon feet. A narrow spindly tail slithers behind as its wings stretch wide, showing the network of veins, muscles, and bones that make up the bat-like wings. A thick brawny neck leads to a lizard-like face, with oversized blue gecko eyes. It shakes its head, and its wings quiver like a bird trying to shake debris from its feathers. Dirt and soot cover the floor of the tunnel, causing Emily to cough.

The dragon takes a step towards her, and Emily turns when she notices the Latovian door coming to life, the cold black steel turning to carved wood.

"You're a Latovian dragon. A real Latovian dragon."

The beast twists its head to the side like an owl before rearing back onto its hind legs. Without warning, it uses one of its front talons to slice open its chest. Warm golden liquid spurts forward, soaking Emily before she can shield herself. Emily's body trembles as she wipes the sticky gold blood from her eyes.

The dragon falls forward, its monstrous legs collapsing beneath it. It nudges Emily with its head, pushing her toward the door before its wings fall, its eyes close, and its chest rises no more.

Emily stifles the urge to cry and places her hand on the Latovian doorknob. Dragon blood coats the door and surrounding wall, and Emily doesn't understand its significance. She looks back at the deceased dragon, saying, "You wanted me to go through. You died so I could go through."

She swallows hard and takes a deep breath, hoping to fill herself with courage. Then she opens the door to Latovia and walks through.

THE TRUTH ABOUT DRAGONS

24

WOLFE STANDS when he sees the portal door transform. He holds his breath, trying to stay calm. He had prepared for this. Well, he had prepared for versions of this. Everything had gone wrong so far. Now he had his people gathered in the main cavern, waiting for word to escape.

Emily enters, her face shell-shocked as golden blood drips from her.

"No," Wolfe gasps. His mouth falls open, and he sucks in a breath, face twisting with the severity of his grief. "Fucking Midnight." His oldest friend had sacrificed himself.

20 YEARS AGO

WOLFE THREW pebbles down the narrow slit of a cave, too tight for an adult. Exploring the caves was more than a hobby for him. He was searching for a way out—a way to escape to a magical land where the outside world wouldn't kill him. There were always rumors that such places existed. He's not stupid enough to believe everything he hears, but he is desperate enough to believe this one.

King Mazilon had already killed Wolfe's family, and now the king seemed to be coming after the orphans. Wolfe couldn't take any more of his friends dying, so here he was searching for hope.

He'd found this path by accident after making a wrong turn. He thought he had seen every part of the caverns, but this one took a lantern as no magic gems lit the way. Lanterns were scarce, especially as an orphan. But Wolfe had come across an abandoned lantern and claimed it as his own, and before he got caught with it, he climbed the ledge that led him down this slanted path.

It moved downward, narrow at the very bottom, but widened into a V shape above his head. It made for an awkward trail. It wasn't much of a trail at all. It was mostly constructed of narrow cliffs with steep drop-offs that had him moving cautiously and clinging to his stolen lantern.

More than once, he wanted to turn back, but he had to keep going. He had to follow through. Surely it had to be this difficult for a reason. There had to be something.

But there wasn't, and after hours of scaling walls and clinging to cliffs, he was too worn out to make the return trip right away.

He slumped awkwardly against a wall and fell asleep.

When he woke, there was nothing but darkness. The fire burned out as he slept, leaving him with an empty lantern and a matchbook with six matches. He slipped out of his jacket, removed his shirt before putting the jacket back on.

He stumbled in the dark, and fell, wedged between the narrow walls. When he righted himself, he ripped his shirt into strands and coiled them around in the lantern by feel. Then he lit it. He took a few steps one direction and then spun back to walk the other way.

Had he really lost his way?

He looked for the markings he made on the rocks but found nothing, and his lantern was already dimming. Everything looked the same here. He was wasting time and precious firelight.

He picked a direction and started jogging, hoping to outlast the light. He knew there were cracks and sharp jutting cliffs the way he had come, and he needed light for those areas. He still had strips of fabric. He'd burn all of his clothes if he had to. If he stayed here, he would die. He kept going after the flames burned out, sure the cliffs were far enough away. He'd light another torch in a moment.

His feet scuffled across the uneven path. And when his foot met nothing but air, he stepped back and lit another strip of fabric. The cavern opened before him, gaping and bottomless.

This was not the way he came. This was something else entirely. He couldn't see the bottom of the cavern even as he dropped the still-lit match. He found a rock and tossed it down, waiting to hear it hit the ground. It surprised him to hear a splash.

Water!

He looked around for a way down or across. He knew he should go back, but what if this was a new water source, or maybe it would lead him back to the caverns he knew. Along the side of the cliff was a narrow ledge that led downward.

He set the lantern on the edge of the cliff and stepped down onto the ledge. He scooted downward, half-scaling the wall. He was halfway down when the light burned out, and the ground below his feet fell away. He plunged downward, arms spiraling as he went below the water's surface with a splash.

He sunk into icy waters, deeper and deeper. He gasped, taking in water as his arms continued to flail. He realized nothing was quite as terrifying as being submerged in deep waters in utter darkness.

Wolfe was not one to panic, which is what kept him alive this long. He exhaled the water, stilled his body until he could determine which way was up. His body started rising on its own, and he followed its lead, swimming to the surface. He gasped, filling his lungs with air as his feet kicked. The cold water made it hard to move, but it was swim or die. He picked a direction and swam until he hit rock. Then he climbed out of the water.

The shivering overtook his whole body, but he had to get out of his clothes. He stripped down, ringing out his clothes before putting them back on.

He was essentially blind in unknown territory. He still had his matches, but they were soaked and would need to dry along with everything else.

He felt around, finding the cavern wall. He sunk against it with chattering teeth and a trembling body. He huddled there, trying to preserve his heat, convinced he would die. He would've cried if it weren't for the sheer panic that overtook him.

He needed to move—to warm up.

He couldn't feel his toes.

It couldn't've been more than forty-five degrees down here. It definitely felt colder. He tried to stand, but he was shaking so violently his limbs wouldn't hold him.

He heard a noise and tried to look, though it was too dark for human sight.

"Hello?" he chattered.

The movement stopped.

"Is su-su-someone th-th-there?"

Then, without a sound, something warm pressed against him. He didn't know what. He didn't care. He was too cold, and wet, and tired to care. This massive thing wrapped around him like a boa constrictor, only it didn't squeeze him. He lifted his head, pressing his frozen nose against its silky fine scales. Its skin was snake-like, but this was no snake. There was only one thing it could be, but they were all dead.

"A dragon," he whispered, and something substantial rested against his head. Then the creature purred, its warm breath falling against his ear.

"Don't eat me," he muttered.

The purring stopped, and its head lifted from his. It let out an irreverent huff, the warm air covering his body.

He wiggled his body closer to the beast. There was not much he could do to outrun a beast this size in the pitch black, so he surrendered to the creature and fell asleep.

Wolfe was nudged awake a while later. The beast was making low grumbling noises as it moved around and disconnected from Wolfe.

Wolfe's clothes were dry, and he was warm. He got to his feet and reached in his pocket, pulling out the matches. They were dry, but it took a few tries to get one to light. Wolfe was thankful he didn't see what had been wrapped around him until now. Otherwise, he would've tried like hell to get away from it.

The beast had a red tint to its smooth scales. It stood at least twelve feet tall on its muscled hind legs. It ruffled two bat-like wings and spread them out to the sides, each one the length of its enormous body. Wolfe held the match in front of him, and the dragon landed on all fours, its front legs only slightly shorter than the back. Its thick neck stretched out and Wolfe saw its liquid amber eyes glow.

Then he saw the others. He only caught a glimpse before the match started burning his fingertips, and he dropped it. He shook his hand, trying to get rid of the pain, and while he focused on that, brilliant blue flames shot to the ceiling of the massive cavern.

Instead of burning out immediately, the flames coalesced, forming a tight ball of light that hung in the center of the cavern. When he could tear his eyes away from the magic ball of fire, Wolfe turned his gaze toward the dragons. There were dozens of them, all of them huge, but their exact sizes varied, though not as drastically as their assortment of colors. The red one that most likely saved his life stepped forward and lowered its lizard-like head. Its skull alone was the size of Wolfe's torso, and its long talons looked as though they could slice him in two without much effort.

The dragon tilted its head and retracted its massive talons as it took another step forward.

"They said you were all dead."

The red dragon dipped its head, and a brilliant blue dragon stepped forward, his eyes blue and sparking. Then he spoke, the dragon's voice both everywhere and nowhere. "It's better if Latovians believe we're dead." The blue dragon steps closer and sniffs at Wolfe. "How old are you, boy?"

"T . . . ten."

"Why didn't you run when you saw Ruby?"

"Who's Ruby."

The dragon tilts its head toward the red dragon.

"Because Ruby saved my life." He looks at Ruby and says, "Thank you."

Ruby dips her head.

Wolfe turns back to the blue dragon. "Are you their leader or something? Why aren't the others talking to me?"

"Because as dragons, we can only bond with one person. Once that bond happens, we can communicate. All the others are already bonded, but their people have all passed away. I am the only dragon who did not bond before we went into hiding."

"You bonded with me? Just now?"

"Yes, don't make me regret our decision. We, as a whole, believe you may be able to help guide Latovia and get it back on track, but you can never tell anyone about us."

"Why are you in hiding?"

"Because Latovia is dying, and we are all that is holding it together. Without us, all of the cave will collapse. Our magic alone keeps it sturdy, but some merciless Latovians started hunting us so they could harness our magic, not knowing or caring that by killing us, they will kill everyone down here. Just ask your king how he got his power."

Wolfe asks, "Why don't you just kill the king?"

"We cannot kill the people we are sworn to protect, our magic forbids it."

"Then you can train me, and I'll kill him."

The dragon makes a hissing noise, and Wolfe realizes he's laughing. "What is your name, boy?"

"Wolfe."

"Wolfe, I have a feeling you'll do much more than just that. I look forward to working together."

"Do you have a name?"

"We only have names, once our bonded human gives us one."

Wolfe looks him over, walking around him, inspecting the shimmering royal blue on his back to the navy tip of his tail. He smiles. "What do you think about Midnight?"

LIES & CURSES

25

EMILY WALKS through the portal into Latovia, immediately feeling the magic of the curse tearing at her subconscious. Then she notices Wolfe waiting for her.

"No," he gasps while she takes in the dragon standing next to him, this one with varying shades of red.

Wolfe's brows pull together and his eyes shine. "Fucking Midnight."

The dragon next to him lowers its head, looking as if it sympathizes with Wolfe.

Anger sparks through her and she steps forward, shouting, "Over and over, we asked you about dragons, and each time, you lied to us! Maybe they were right to lock you down here. Everything that comes out of here is an abomination. You've turned Ashley into a monster, and your magic is running rampant in Latovia's dead, turning their rotting corpses into fire breathing demons."

Wolfe stands straighter. "Once you lift the curse, we will help you defeat the wild magic."

"I don't think I want the kind of help you offer. It always comes with a catch. The only reason I came here was because of that dragon—"

"Midnight," Wolfe corrects. "Use his name. He sacrificed himself to save you, and to save Latovia."

Emily is too angry to show compassion. "Did you sic Ashley on us?"

"I let her out of Latovia, knowing she would come for you, but it was that or let all my people die. Latovia wouldn't have lasted the night with the power she'd amassed, and it's easier for the magic to hide from us down here. It can't hide above ground, and I knew it'd go after power. Latovian dragons—real Latovian dragons can stop the wild magic. We just need you to release us from our cage."

Emily feels the pressure of Latovian magic, the pull of it, the whispers, but pushes through. "If I free you, what's to say you won't all become what Ashley is right now?"

"Wild magic is greedy," Wolfe explains. "It will take and take because the only thing it desires is more power. Dragons are the opposite. They were created from magic to protect the people. Not just Latovian people, but all people."

"What about the rumors about them burning villages to the ground? They were the reason you closed Latovia in the first place."

"It was a Latovian with wild magic that burned those villages, and Latovia needed protecting from the outside world. Not the other way around."

Emily raises her voice, "Why couldn't you have just told us this?"

"We are running out of time, Emily. Lift the curse!"

"You don't get to demand anything of me."

"The hell I don't. I'm about to save your ass. And I'm not letting another dragon sacrifice themselves because of your temper tantrum."

The magic's pull on her grows. "I saw what the magic did to Wendy. I don't want that done to other children in the world because I free your kind."

"That's exactly what you're doing by keeping us here."

As they stare at one another, Emily asks, "And what will happen to Ashley?"

Wolfe answers, "I don't know. We'll save her if we can. If the magic doesn't kill her."

The pull is growing too overwhelming, so before she is taken under by its power, she lets out a burst of energy. Her hand reaches for the wall, and when it connects, white flames tear their way up the wall and spread rapidly.

Fire runs a line down the ceiling of every cave, tunnel, and cavern. Emily feels her power spread. She feels the network of caves unravel in her mind like a map. And with it, she feels every Latovian, every heartbeat—every life—from the cluster of orphans, to the gathering families, and even the dozens of Latovian dragons. She feels it all.

The curse rescinds and the fire dies without harming a soul. White ash falls on them from above, looking like snow.

Wolfe steps forward. "You did it."

She feels a sense of renewed purpose now that she felt every person she's fighting for. "Yes, now let's go!" She takes a step toward the portal door but stops when Wolfe says, "Emily, this is Ruby." He gestures to the dragon. "She saved my life once." As soon as the words are out of his mouth, he begins convulsing.

Emily tries not to panic. "Wolfe?"

She soon realizes it's more than a seizure. His arms elongate, his skin changes tone, his bone structure churns beneath his skin. Magic.

Emily steps back, mouth gaping as Wolfe stands before her, a shimmering navy dragon, with blood-red eyes. "Holy, shit!"

Dragon Wolfe lowers his head and then, with his giant taloned paw, nudges Emily to climb onto the red dragon's back—Ruby's back.

As she does, Wolfe smashes through the portal wall and into the underground tunnel. A yellow dragon zooms out right behind Wolfe and Emily rides the red dragon through, holding on for dear life as it flies up through the narrow hole Midnight had created.

LATOVIAN DRAGONS

26

High above the lake, Patrick hovers in the middle of a waterspout vortex. His head is pounding, his concussion weakening him, but it doesn't keep him from using all the strength and powers he can conjure to lash out at the purple scaled dragon that attacked Emily.

Unlike the other creatures, the scaled beast seems to have merged with Ashley instead of consuming and destroying her like the others. It is using Ashley's power to fight back as it tries to go down the hole Emily seemingly created.

Using their Olvasho gifts, he and Lathe work together to distract and contain the dragon. Alec and Morgan stay hidden in the trees by the edge of the lake where Alec is trying to connect with Ashley.

Jerrick is still unaccounted for, but Patrick doesn't have time to think about that as the dragon shifts into a giant mass of magic, going after all of them at once.

Magic smothers Lathe, pinning him to the ground while

Patrick's water cyclone gets hit by a supernatural electrical current. He loses grip of his gifts and free-falls.

Something catches him tight around his ankle and lowers him to the ground. When he rolls up to his feet, he watches dragons coming out of the hole in the ground. There are six in total, and he sees Emily riding on the back of a red one.

The dragons swarm the mass of magic that had consumed Ashley. The magic appears to recoil, cowering from the dragons. A navy dragon lands next to Lathe, and the magic pulls away, freeing Lathe. To Patrick's surprise, Lathe climbs onto the back of the dragon without hesitation.

The magic shifts its form and the purple dragon reemerges. Seeing that it's surrounded, it fights back like a savage, using everything at its disposal. It uproots trees and chucks them through the air. It sets the grass on fire, making it harder to fight. It even plucks the deformed dragons it made out of the sky to throw at the Latovian dragons.

Deja witnesses the Latovian dragons come from the ground looking majestic. They are not bulky or clumsy like the imposter dragons. They are agile and swift—mystic beauties against the starry backdrop. She watches as they swarm the purple scaled beast, and even as it catches the grass on fire and lobs trees at the dragons, Deja knows they are rescued.

She smells something foul and turns just in time to see a giant deformed praying mantis looking creature coming at her, not from the sky, but on foot. She tries to dodge it, but it's right behind her. One of its spindled legs knocks her to the ground and stabs at her. She rolls away, but the creature's sharp bony leg pierces through her calf. Deja screams, trying to pull away, but she's pinned to the ground.

She covers her face and curls into a ball as another spindled leg comes at her torso.

From the corner of her eye, she catches movement. Maggie leaps up, tearing at the creature's throat and throws it off balance. The beast stumbles away from Deja, and the bone stabbing through her calf snaps off as the creature falls.

Maggie is still tearing at its throat when the creature knocks her away. Maggie yelps as she flies backward. The creature stands up, its head dangling by a single tendon. It staggers forward before tumbling to the ground in a heap of decaying flesh.

With the deformed creature's bone still protruding out of her leg, Deja crawls over to where Maggie lays panting heavily. Deja tries to staunch the bleeding, but the dog has been pierced through the chest.

The pool of blood grows around her, and Deja knows there is nothing she can do. If she were older, she might be able to save her, but she is still too young to hold the sun's power. And there is not enough time for anyone else to get to them.

She strokes Maggie's face, saying soothing words—words of praise—words of gratitude. It should be Deja lying there dying, not Maggie.

EMILY FEELS IT—A tearing sensation through her chest, like a piece of her is being ripped away.

"Maggie!" she cries, looking back over her shoulder as she clings to the airborne dragon. "No," she sobs.

She has to get to her. She has to save her dog—her protector. She tries to turn her dragon around, but they can't stop what they're doing. It's too important, and their hold on the wild magic is tenuous at best. Even if she were to pull away, she knows she won't make it in time to save her.

She keeps trying to catch a glimpse, her hair streaking across her face as she looks back towards Deja and Maggie. Deja's body drapes over the dog, and Emily knows it's already too late.

She lets out a scream of anguish and pours her magic into Ruby. The dragon, in turn, moves faster, and Emily explodes the tree sailing at them through the air. They dive through the confetti wood shavings, and Ruby's talons latch onto the wild magic, ripping the purple dragon's wing clean off.

Lathe didn't question why Wolfe's voice came out of the navy dragon. He just did as instructed, climbing on the winged demon with glowing red-eyes.

Wolfe explained a few things, like the fact that wild magic can't be destroyed. There is no way to get rid of it, but it can be transformed into something else, which is why the Latovian dragons are so important. Because they have the ability to absorb wild magic without turning into crazed power-hungry lunatics, like Ashley, for example.

His beautiful fiancée was mad with power. It wasn't

really her, and he couldn't reach her, so he told Wolfe to get a dragon to pick up Alec.

Alec doesn't look thrilled to be riding on the back of a dragon, but the yellow beast forced him into getting on.

Lathe shouts to Alec. "Can you reach her?"

"Not well!"

"Try to get her to give the magic away. If they have to take the last of it from her, she may not survive."

Patrick and Morgan run over the grassy hill, hiding behind a strategically landscaped row of trees. Trees the purple dragon hadn't ripped from the ground.

The breeze picks up a nasty stench and carries it toward them just as they come across a hive of foul creatures made from magic. Patrick gags, while Morgan tucks her nose into her shirt.

There are nearly fifty wingless creatures, only slightly larger than humans.

Morgan elbows Patrick. "Look, there's Jerrick."

A few of the creatures are in the middle of spinning Jerrick's unconscious body into a cocoon-like web.

She asks, "Can you save any of them?"

Patrick looks over the warped corpses moving around as if they are still alive, but the magic alone animates their movements. Most of their organs have been destroyed, and Patrick is relieved no one survived the twisting of their organs and bending of their bones.

Patrick pulls on his gifts, carrying a stream of water from the lake. He sends a steady trickle through the grass up ahead while he says, "There is no life here aside from Jerrick. You should look away now. You won't want to see what I'm about to do."

Morgan spins away. "Let me know when it's over."

"It should be quick." Patrick separates the water into hundreds of dime-sized droplets and forms them into spearheads.

The trickle of water he sent ahead, raises like a shield around Jerrick's body. The creatures working on him become curious, and before they can call attention to it, Patrick hurls the hundreds of water droplets forward with rocket force.

Once the water bullets hit their targets, they explode, causing maximum damage to the creatures. Some scream, others don't get the chance. Most of their bodies crumple instantly, and the magic leaves the broken unsalvageable corpses.

Only a few survive the assault, so Patrick sends additional rounds. None of the creatures survive the second attack. He gathers the water, moving the bodies into a heap on the far side, away from Jerrick.

"It's done," he says to Morgan as he massages his head. The surge of power made his concussion worse. "I'm going to sit down for a moment," he warns before falling over.

He's thankful Morgan doesn't ask if he's okay while she helps him to the ground. "You stay here. I'm going to see if I can detangle Jerrick."

He has just enough energy to nod as the world spins. He'd pushed himself too far.

The next thing he knows, Jerrick is kneeling in front of him while Morgan shines a light in his eyes.

THE WILD MAGIC WEAKENS, but Lathe isn't sure Alec is getting through to Ashley. He didn't seem to be making any progress as Ashley lies on the ground. The magic repairs her signature bleach blonde locks back to their original dark chestnut waves. A purple haze surrounds her, and the wild magic still fights, but the dragons stand around her, absorbing the deadly power.

Through their connection, Wolfe says to Lathe, "We've been out of Latovia for too long, and the dragons down there don't have enough power to hold it together. They're trying to get the people out, but they have no voice to explain, so everyone is panicking. It's bound to collapse any minute.

Just then, Morgan, Jerrick, and Patrick come over the hill.

Lathe says, "I'm not leaving her, but what if we send them down to explain."

"That could work."

Lathe slides off the dragon's back and runs to meet his friends at the bottom of the hill.

LATHE APPROACHES them as they reach the bottom of the hill. "Jerrick, you okay?"

"Yeah, they just put me under some sort of trance. I'm better now, but he's not." Jerrick points to Patrick.

Morgan says, "He's barely standing. He's been fighting with a concussion this whole time. He needs to rest."

Patrick confirms this when he sits in the grass and lays back.

Lathe explains what he needs, and Jerrick and Morgan help Patrick into the house before traveling down to Latovia. The tunnel is crumbling at one end, where the dragon made a hole to the surface.

The portal door is gone. Instead, there is a giant black hole in the wall. They step around the dead dragon and try to avoid stepping in its golden blood.

"I can't imagine this will go over well when the Latovians come through."

Morgan nods, and then with breath held, she steps through the black hole and finds herself standing in a cave. Jerrick comes through right behind her. "He said they gathered everyone in the main cavern. Do you know where that is?"

THE IMAGES BURN through Alec's brain. *Ashley touching Lathe's skin for the first time, the time he met her at the bar, him finally giving in. Ashley wrapped in Lathe's arms. Her engagement ring turning purple. Her picture of their life together.*

"Ashley, fight for him," Alec speaks in her mind.

Her voice comes to him. "I can't. It's too strong."

"Just let go of the magic." Alec says, "You have to separate."

He feels her fighting it.

"Just let it go."

"It's part of who I am."

"It's not all of who you are."

Lathe wishes he knew if Alec was getting through to her, but he doesn't want to interrupt his concentration by asking.

Wolfe warns, "This is taking too long."

"Relax," Lathe says, they're clearing Latovia. Give her a little more time."

Now that they have this under control, Wolfe releases three of the six dragons. All three dive back toward Latovia, leaving only Ruby, the red dragon Emily is riding, and Rex, the yellow beast Alec is perched on.

Lathe stands at Wolfe's side, waiting to run forward when they're finished.

Blood-red eyes turn to him. "She has thirty seconds before we pull the rest of it out of her."

Lathe swallows.

BITTERSWEET

27

As THE DRAGONS pull the remaining wild magic from Ashley, Emily senses Latovia collapsing, but there are people still inside. "Wolfe!" she shouts. "We need to go. They haven't gotten everyone out."

Sensing the change, Alec slips off of Rex, and the yellow dragon takes off.

Lathe runs toward Ashley when Wolfe pulls away. The navy dragon dives into the tunnel after Rex. Ruby, and Emily follow.

They get to the underground tunnel and find it empty aside from Rex who is setting Midnight's body on fire.

Emily says, "Where is everyone?"

Wolfe dives right through the gaping black hole in the wall, and Ruby and Emily trail behind.

Dust and rocks fall from the cave ceiling as they zoom through the tunnels. They get to the main cavern and Latovians are scattered everywhere. At the center, there is a heated debate surrounding Morgan and Jerrick. Wolfe and Ruby land next to them.

Emily asks, "What's going on?"

"They think we're lying. They don't trust us or the dragons."

Wolfe's body shifts on the spot, his lower half covered by his own dragon skin when he transforms to man. People gasp and his voice booms. "The curse is broken, and Latovia is dead. Get out unless you want to be buried alive."

He transforms back into a full dragon and grabs people with his talons, carrying them out through the portal. All the dragons seem to follow suit. But Emily pauses. "Ruby, there are orphans the other way."

Ruby continues to fly toward the exit, so Emily jumps off the dragon. Using the air to soften her fall, Emily runs against the current of Latovians.

She finds Morgan standing out of the crowd on top of a boulder. Emily jumps up next to her, an inhuman move. "Morgan, what are you doing?"

"Jerrick put me up here and told me to wave down a dragon, so I didn't get crushed in the stampede. What are you doing? Why'd you give up your dragon?"

"There are kids that way," She points away from the exit. I've gotta get them out."

"I'm going with you."

"Okay, hold on." Emily uses her gifts to carry them over the crowd.

"Oh, this is weird," Morgan complains with nervous laughter.

Once they're in the clear, Morgan and Emily run together. Larger rocks fall, and Emily diverts the stones that would fall on top of them. They find the kids bundled together, hiding in a notch in the cave wall.

There are four girls, all of them under six years old. Emily kneels. "Hey, girls. I'm Emily, and this is Morgan. We're friends of the king. We need you to come with us so we can help you out of here."

The girls don't move right away, and one of them says, "But there are dragons out there."

"These dragons are helping us." Emily reaches out a hand. "Come on."

One of the girls takes her hand, and they all slowly unfold from their hiding spot. Emily picks up the two-year-old, carrying her on her hip while the others hold hands with her and Morgan.

"It's this way." They move, and Emily continues deflecting the falling stones. They make it out to the now empty main cavern before the whole cavern shakes, and a car-sized hunk falls in front of them. Emily hands Morgan the little girl, so she can use both hands to deflect the boulders that could crush them.

They are running as fast as they can through the stadium-sized cavern when a house-sized chunk falls toward them, and Emily holds it off, suspending it in the air, so it doesn't block their exit. Her arms tremble with the amount of energy it takes to hold. She looks up and forces the massive rock to the side.

She looks back to the girls just in time to see a boulder headed straight for them. With a burst of wind, she shoves Morgan and the girls out of the way. She doesn't see the giant sheet of rock headed for her until all she can do is dive out of the way.

She cries out as pain erupts in her right leg, the boulder crushing it. She's afraid to look, knowing it's serious.

Morgan hesitates at the mouth of the tunnel that leads to the mansion.

"Keep going," she yells to Morgan and the kids with her.

"Can you lift it?" Morgan shouts back.

"Go!"

Morgan looks around like she's not sure what to do, but after the brief hesitation, she lifts two of the kids into her arms and they run.

Lathe pulls Ashley's body into his lap, cradling her. Alec stays close, and Lathe knows he's trying to give them privacy but, at the same time, wanting to know if Ashley will wake up.

She's alive, and Lathe clings to that as he holds her. Her eyes eventually flutter open, and after looking up and seeing him, she turns her face into his chest and sobs.

Lathe cries too, unable to hold it all in for another second. He was so afraid he lost her, and it hurts him to see her this way. He rocks her for several moments before she pulls back.

"Lathe, they took it. They took all the magic."

"I know. You're better now."

"No," she sobs, holding up her left hand to show him the diamond engagement ring. "They took it all."

The bright diamond doesn't show a hint of purple, and Lathe understands what she's saying. They didn't just take the wild magic; they took her magic.

"Why?" Lathe asks.

"The magic was too intertwined. If I wanted to live, I had to let it all go."

He holds her tighter, saying, "Thank you for letting it go. I don't ever want to lose you."

Ashley hiccups and opens her mouth to speak when Alec interrupts. "Uh, guys. Is that Deja?"

They look over into the meadow where Lathe's snow-white horse is kneeling on the ground next to the girl.

They stand, and Ashley pushes Lathe away. "Go."

Lathe jumps up, carried by the wind across the field. He lands by the deformed creature and walks toward Deja, trying to figure out what had happened here. Deja sits with her back resting against the mare, who seems to be the only one who had time to comfort the child. Deja's legs are out in front of her, her left calf seriously injured. A few feet away. Deja's jacket drapes across Maggie, only her feet peeking out from under the dragon skin.

"It's my fault," Deja cries, staring at Maggie.

Lathe shakes his head and sits next to her in the mud. "How is this your fault?"

"I didn't see that thing coming. She had to protect me. She saved my life, and I could do nothing to save her."

"This isn't your fault."

"Emily is going to be devastated."

Lathe nods. "She will be sad, but I think if she were in Maggie's shoes, she would've done the same thing Maggie did. She would protect you no matter the cost. Now let me look at your leg."

THE SHOCK BLOCKS some of the pain, but it's still debilitating. Emily's arms give out and she falls to the ground, tears falling on the dusty floor. The floor cracks and splinters like ice. Emily gathers herself and twists, looking at her lower right leg crushed beneath the boulder. She tries to lift it with no luck, so she moves to plan B. Flames jet out of her hand, and she cuts into the rock, cutting at it bit by bit as boulders fall from the ceiling. She pulls her leg free, screaming with the pain.

She struggles to get to her feet, and once she succeeds, she hops forward, yelping in pain. She's not going to make it. She knocks away another boulder that falls, but it's too painful to move. Her vision goes blurry, the agony in her leg making her delirious.

Talons grab her torso. Her feet leave the ground. She soars through the crumbling cave tunnels, fighting against the pain.

Fighting, fighting, fighting the pull to lose consciousness. They soar out of Latovia and into the tunnel below the mansion. It's packed with people, some of them injured, all of them in shock.

She spots Morgan with the girls she was carrying. She looks as though she's about to go in looking for Emily, then she spots her. The dragon sets her down gently, but she collapses anyway. As she lies on the floor, looking up at the curved brick ceiling, the pain and exhaustion pull her under.

PATRICK MANAGES to ease the pain, but her leg is crushed and hanging limp, too complex for him to heal.

She wakes only minutes after losing consciousness and looks up at him, tears in her eyes. "I thought you were supposed to be resting?" she asks with a smirk.

"I knew you'd do something suicidal without me. I came down, and sure enough, no one knew where you were. Wolfe went back in after you."

She lifts her hand to his cheek. "We did it."

He wipes away her tears, his eyes soften, and he smiles. "We did. We made it."

Despite the agony, it's a tender moment, one she won't forget.

A grating noise pulls Patrick's attention over her head. His face goes slack as his eyes widen.

"What is it?"

Patrick doesn't answer, instead, his head swivels to one side, then the other as groans and screams erupt all over the tunnel. "This is going to be a problem."

Emily props herself up onto her elbows, her mouth falling open as she witnesses dozens of Latovian bodies shifting. Their clothes rip as bones rearrange beneath their skin that thickens with glossy scales.

Emily whispers, "They're shifting into dragons."

Those who aren't shifting are attempting to stop their loved ones from turning. Some are shouting and grabbing at their loved one's deformed bodies while others back away in stunned silence.

Patrick stands, looking through the chaos. "Where is Wolfe?"

Wolfe lands right next to them, with a man's body but the wings and tail of a dragon. Before they can ask him what's going on, Wolfe says, "There is a lot to explain, but right now I need to take my winged friends out of here before something bad happens. I'll be back later for everyone else."

"Do you have somewhere to take them?"

"Yeah, there is an abandoned airfield ten miles from here. I've been getting it ready for years."

"That's where you've been disappearing to. Why didn't you tell us?"

"I didn't know how this would play out. I still don't, but this was a team effort, and I appreciate everything you've done for my people. I will be back soon."

Wolfe goes full dragon and gathers the rest of his fully formed winged friends before grabbing the shifting bodies and carrying them out of the tunnel.

AS THE SUN RISES

28

WOLFE COMES BACK for the rest of his people, and they gather the bodies from the battle, building a bonfire.

Lathe had taken the horse back to the barn and tried to convince Deja to let him move Maggie, but she refused. She still sits in the middle of the meadow with Maggie.

Wolfe lands next to her and shifts into human form to sit next to her. "I'm relieved it wasn't you," Wolfe speaks. "I've been distracted with worry over whether or not you were okay. I forget that you're eight, because you've never acted eight, but I think you should. And Emily isn't upset with you, she has a shattered leg and can't make it out here. She's on the patio. I think we should take Maggie to her."

EMILY SITS in a chair on the patio, her shattered leg propped up. She refuses to go to the hospital until this was done, so for now she's doped up on morphine and Patrick continues to relieve as much pain as possible.

She looks out to the Latovian people gathered on the back lawn. Most of them have nothing but the clothes on their backs. Their lives have been displaced and only a few thought to pack a bag, and even they don't have more than a satchel's worth. She feels for them and sees them as her people even though they likely don't see themselves that way.

Some Latovians are gathering bodies while others are basking in the sliver of moonlight. She feels their magic growing and if she wasn't so doped up, she might worry whether they would turn on the people who helped them.

For now, she's just relieved her friends survived. All of them, except for the one Wolfe is carrying towards her now. She swallows as the tears blur her vision. Deja follows slightly behind Wolfe, her face tilted down.

As they arrive in front of her, Patrick's hands land on Emily's shoulders, lending his support, but she knows he loved Maggie like his own.

Maggie is covered by Deja's dragon skin jacket, but she sees her paws hanging out and bites her lip when it begins to tremble.

"Deja?" Emily calls.

Deja looks up when her name is called, but she's still hiding behind Wolfe.

"Come here," Emily says.

Deja steps around Wolfe, glancing up at him. He gives her a nod of encouragement as she moves to stand in front of Emily, saying, "I'm so sor—"

Emily uses the wind to pull her closer and she hugs Deja, whispering, "I'm so glad you're safe."

Deja stiffens in her arms, but Emily doesn't let go. "Maggie was the best dog and I'm going to miss her a lot, but she chose to fight for you, Deja, and I'm proud of her for that. What happened to her is not your fault."

Deja's arms go around Emily as she cries into her shoulder.

When she pulls back, Wolfe lays the dog next to Emily and says, "While we're getting everyone acclimated to this new life, could some of our children stay here at the estate?"

"Of course," Emily says. "I might have to stay at the hospital for a few nights."

"I'll run it by Jerrick."

"Run what by me?" Jerrick says, coming from inside the house.

"Some of the orphans staying here."

Jerrick nods, pulling out his phone. "Sure, let me order bunk beds."

Wolfe turns to Deja. "You should stay here."

"But—"

With a headshake, he says, "I'm not arguing. You need to act your age for once in your life. I'm ordering you to stay here." He kneels down. "It's not because I'm upset with you. It's because it's what's right."

She hugs him.

ASHLEY AND WOLFE meet up when he's finished talking to Emily. She approaches him. "Thank you for pulling it out of me."

Wolfe nods. "You finally got what you wanted, princess. A normal life with the man you love, free from our brutal Latovian ways."

She presses her lips together with a sigh. "I don't know. I think I might kinda, like miss some of it, maybe." She smiles. "You're a great leader, Wolfe. Your people are lucky to have you."

Lathe approaches. "Good luck with the transition. You know we're here if you need anything."

"I do." He gives Lathe a hug and kisses Ashley's cheek before walking towards the pile of deformed bodies his people started gathering.

Ashley spots Morgan and Alec sitting on the hill overlooking the back of the estate. She grabs Lathe's hand, and they meet up with them on the hill.

Ashley sits in the grass next to Alec and Lathe sits on her other side. As the sun peeks over the horizon, Ashley says, "Well, this is going to be a landscaping disaster."

"For us, maybe," Alec says. "But not for them. They'll just wave their hand around and it will all go back to the way it was."

Lathe laughs. "That's not how it works."

Ashley stays quiet. Alec had grouped her in with *us* and it reminds her she is no longer special. Her magic is gone. She feels stupid about being upset over it because she has only known about her magic for a few months, but now to go on without it feels like a huge loss.

Before Lathe notices her mood change, she jokes, "Wait

a minute, does this mean I get out of doing work now that my magic is gone?"

As the sun rises, all of the Latovians congregate around the deformed bodies they gathered. Wolfe, in his dragon form, sets it on fire. The blaze burns hotter than usual and once there is nothing but ash, Wolfe gathers the Latovians to lead them to their new home.

Stay Tuned!

The conclusion of the Valla Series coming 2021.

Book Five ~ Blood in the Roots

ACKNOWLEDGMENTS

Thank you for continuing to follow Emily's story.

It's no secret that I cut it way too close with this book. It was a race to complete it on time, and I felt overwhelmed with the support I received. It is a huge blessing to have a team of people excited to read along as I write and who are willing to critique my work. You guys are my superheroes!

Cathy, this book was painful to write without you. You were so much a part of this story and it breaks my heart you weren't physically here to finish it with me. I still have your voice in my head and there were several times I laughed to myself while editing those stupid typos. You knew what was going to happen in this book before I wrote it. Thank you for all your guidance.

To my mom, thank you for always having my back, even when I drop the ball and have to scramble at the last minute. You are always so encouraging. Thank you for pushing me.

Melissa Di Rienzo I can't thank you enough for being with me as I struggled through this book. Your feedback and brainstorming sessions made this book work. I feel so lucky to have you. I love you, girl!

A huge thank you to Tim Rezes who has such a keen eye. I really couldn't ask for a better father-in-law. Thank you for being excited about these books!

To all of my sisters, thank you for your feedback and following this story.

To my husband, thank you for letting me spoil this story for you. You've been so amazing this past year with all the emotions. Even with the stress, excitement, and grief, you were there to support me. Remember the time you spent forty-five minutes helping nail down mental health issues for the magically inclined. I won the husband lotto, and I know it.

ABOUT THE AUTHOR

Anna Rezes has been passionate about writing since she was a child. When she's not busy honing her superpowers or traveling to other worlds full of fictional characters, she is spending time with family and friends. She lives in Central Ohio with her husband, their two dogs, and the cat they love and hate. Anna is the author of *Unraveling Emily, Descendant of Valla, Guardian of Latovia, The Thorn, Broken Alliance*, and *Pink f*cking Moscato*.

For more from Anna Rezes visit:
www.annarezes.com
www.instagram.com/anna_rezes

www.facebook.com/annarezesauthor
www.twitter.com/annarezes

Pink f*cking Moscato